I0663892

FOUL PLAY AND FIGGY PUDDING

NAOMI GREER

Edited by
TERESA H. CARROLL

Welcome to Butternut Cove
MONDAY, DECEMBER 15TH.
TEN DAYS UNTIL CHRISTMAS.

In Butternut Cove, even the crumbs tell a tale…

Faye Harper stood at Sweet Cliffs observation point, her Dane, Tiny, pressed warm against her leg. His pedigree papers read: Sir Wellington of Winterwind, Registered Great Dane— but to everyone in Butternut Cove, including the mailman and possibly the mayor, he was just *Tiny*.

She tucked a loose strand of windblown brunette hair behind her ear and watched seabirds soar against the pale morning sky. The ocean stretched endlessly before her, grey-green and restless, and for a moment she let herself simply breathe.

Today marked five years.

Five years since the car accident that took Derek and Jenny.

Most days, the grief settled over her like a quiet shadow. Today, it sliced through her, sharp as the December wind on bare skin.

Tiny leaned harder against her, sensing the shift in her mood the way he always did. She rested her hand on his massive head. He was brindle-colored—soft cedar bark tones mixed with winter shadow.

He shifted slightly, pressing closer in a way that said:

Stay. I've got you.

"I'm fine," she murmured, though no one had asked. "Let's go open the café."

A gust of wind sent a loose scrap of paper tumbling across the path. Faye frowned and stooped to pick it up, expecting a receipt or grocery list.

Two words stared back at her in jagged handwriting:

Lot 47.

At first, she pulled a small laugh from habit—one of those automatic *nothing to see here* reactions.

But then came the chill.

Something about this morning felt... different. She tucked the paper into her pocket without examining it further. Probably nothing. She had enough to think about today.

Her watch vibrated with a notification. Time to open.

"Come on, honey."

Faye and Tiny walked back to her Jeep. His massive frame moving with surprising grace. He hopped into the back seat—the only place he fit—and they drove the short distance to Main Street.

WHEN FAYE STEPPED inside *The Heirloom Table Café*, the warm scent of baked goods and spiced chai wrapped around her like a comforting embrace. The exposed brickwork, rustic furnishings, and rotating displays of period maps gave the café a historic ambiance. That made customers feel like they'd stepped into another era.

"Morning, Faye!" Tessa Martinez called from the kitchen, already elbow-deep in prep work.

Faye shook off the cold and managed a smile. "I see you beat me here. Again."

Tessa emerged with a steaming cup and pressed it into Faye's hands. Chai, made exactly the way you like it. "I know today isn't easy," Tessa said quietly, wrapping her in a brief hug. "So I wanted to be here. To help."

"You don't have to."

"I know I don't have to. I want to. That's what sisters do."

Sisters-in-law, technically. Faye had married Derek Martin; Tessa had married his twin brother Alan. They'd both become widows before thirty-five, and somewhere in that shared grief, they'd become family in a way that went deeper than marriage certificates.

"Thank you," Faye said, and deeply felt it, even as something in her resisted the care. She was fine. She could handle today. She could handle anything.

The back door swung open, letting in a gust of December air and the sound of cheerful barking. Callie Sweet breezed in, a basket of fresh bread hooked over one arm and a golden retriever padding at her heels. In a carrier on her shoulder rode her Siamese cat, that surveyed the café with imperious blue eyes.

"Morning delivery!" Callie announced, setting the basket on the counter. The bread was still warm, the crust crackling. "Sourdough, rosemary focaccia, and that olive loaf you love."

"You're a lifesaver," Faye said, already reaching for the focaccia. "This is what makes my grilled cheese legendary."

Callie grinned, her warmth filling the room. She had that

3

effect on people—a natural brightness that made everyone around her feel a little lighter. "I know. That's why I'm here at 7 A.M." She glanced at the figgy pudding molds lining the counter. "Big week. You ready for the competition?"

"Ready as I'll ever be."

The Siamese let out a delicate meow from her carrier.

"*Bonjour, tout le monde,*" Callie translated with a wink. "Fig says good morning."

Jaxson, Callie's golden retriever, had already found Tiny and the two dogs were engaged in their usual ritual of mutual sniffing and tail wagging. Despite the size difference—Tiny towered over Jaxson—they'd been friends since Callie returned to Butternut Cove three years ago.

"Have you heard from Gert?" Faye asked. Callie's grandmother had practically raised her after... well, after.

Something flickered across Callie's face—there and gone. "Oh, you know Gert. Off sailing the Mediterranean with her friends. Living her best life." She said it lightly, but Faye caught the undertone. Gert's sudden departure six months ago had been unexpected, and Callie still seemed puzzled by it.

"Well, give her my love when you hear from her."

"Will do." Callie shouldered her now-empty basket. "I'd better get back. Saturday's orders are piling up, and I've got three celebration cakes to finish before the Ball." She paused at the door. "You okay? You seem..."

"I'm fine," Faye said automatically.

Callie held her gaze a moment longer than necessary, then nodded. "Okay. But you know where to find me if you need anything."

Callie left, picking up Fig in her carrier and Jaxson following close behind, Faye caught Tessa watching her with that knowing look.

"What?"

"Nothing. Just... you know you can talk to me, right? About today. About anything."

"I know." Faye turned back to the figgy pudding. "But right now, I need to focus on not burning these. The Victorian Ball is Saturday, and I refuse to let Kent Blake's pudding outshine mine."

Tessa let it go, but Faye felt her sister-in-law's concern like a weight on her shoulders. She didn't need concern. She needed to work.

⸺

BY MID-MORNING, the café hummed with its usual Monday rhythm. Locals stopping for coffee and Faye's signature grilled cheese—sharp cheddar and caramelized onion on Callie's rosemary focaccia, paired with a spiced chai. Tourists wandering in from the harbor, charmed by the Christmas decorations and the scent of cinnamon.

The bell above the door chimed as Peter Grayson stepped in. He ran an antique shop a few streets off Main, and he'd been a regular at *The Heirloom Table Café* since Faye opened three years ago.

He picked up a box of Faye's snickerdoodles, "For my restoration clients," Peter said, lifting the box with a polite smile. "Nothing impresses like your cookies, Faye."

He grabbed a sample of Christmas cookies as he headed out the door.

"Tell Luke I said hello," she called after him.

"Will do."

Is there something special going on with that Detective cousin of mine? He said mockingly.

The door swung shut behind him.

From the back, Noel—her delivery boy—emerged with a stack of empty crates. He was seventeen, gangly and good-natured, and he'd been making runs for Faye since his sophomore year.

"That's my last load before I head out," he said, setting the crates by the door. "Visiting my grandparents in Vermont for Christmas. Back on the 26th."

"Safe travels, Noel. We'll miss you."

"Thanks, Ms. Harper. Save me some figgy pudding?"

"If there's any left after Kent Blake and I battle it out."

Noel grinned and headed out. Through the window, Faye watched him pause to chat with Peter Grayson on the sidewalk. Peter said something, gestured toward the harbor, and Noel nodded before they parted ways.

Faye turned back to her work, thinking nothing of it.

▭

FROM THE BACK KITCHEN DOOR, Dixie Martin burst into the room, all sixteen-year-old energy and bouncing curls.

"Hey, Aunt Faye! Morning!" She darted forward and wrapped Faye in a brief but fierce hug. "School's closed—water pipe burst. So I'm helping today!"

"That's what I hear." Faye smiled at her niece—Tessa and Alan's daughter, who'd been living with Faye for the past few months. The bungalow outside town was too isolated for a teenager who thrived on activity, and Faye's house on Ocean Street put Dixie in the heart of everything. "While you're at it, would you refresh Tiny's water? And maybe take him out back for a few minutes?"

"On it!" Dixie crouched to hug the Dane, who accepted the attention with dignified patience. "Come on, big guy. Let's go."

As Dixie led Tiny toward the back door, Tessa appeared at Faye's elbow.

"She's good for you," Tessa said quietly. "Having her here is a help."

"She's good for the café," Faye deflected. "Extra hands during the holiday rush."

"That's not what I meant and you know it."

Faye didn't answer. She focused on arranging the sugar cookies in the display case, each one a perfect little work of art.

⸺

JUST BEFORE NOON, the café door swung open and a gust of cold air swept through. Faye's heart did a small, traitorous skip as she recognized the silhouette.

"Detective Luke Grayson," she said, keeping her voice light. "To what do I owe the pleasure?"

Luke shook snow from his coat, revealing the peppered stubble that made him look ruggedly handsome in a way Faye absolutely refused to think about. "Just checking in. Making sure you're not stirring up trouble."

"Me? Trouble?" She pressed a hand to her chest in mock offense. "I'm just a humble café owner making grilled cheese."

"Mm-hmm." His blue eyes crinkled with amusement. "How's the holiday prep going?"

"Chaotic. The Ball is Saturday, and I've got approximately one thousand figgy puddings to make between now and then."

"I heard Kent Blake entered the competition."

"News travels fast."

"Small town." Luke accepted the coffee Tessa handed him with a grateful nod. "You doing okay? I know today is..." He trailed off, suddenly awkward.

"I'm fine," Faye said, the words automatic now. How many times had she said them today? "Busy. That helps."

Luke studied her a moment, and she had the uncomfortable feeling that he saw more than she wanted him to. "Well," he said finally, "if you need anything—"

"I know where to find you."

The door burst open before either of them could say more, bringing in a gust of icy wind. A figure stumbled through, bundled in layers. It was Rose Fairweather—a frantic, familiar face and far from her usual composed self. The associate archivist always carried an air of elegance that never quite fit in Butternut Cove.

"Faye! You won't believe—" Rose stopped short, noticing Luke. "Oh. Detective. I didn't realize you were here."

"Just leaving." Luke set down his coffee cup. "Faye. Tessa." He nodded to each of them, then to Rose, and slipped out the door.

Rose barely waited for it to close. "Kent Blake," she announced, as if the name itself were an accusation. "He's entered a figgy pudding in the Ball competition. He's telling everyone his will be the best Butternut Cove has ever seen."

"I heard."

"You should withdraw. No one wants two figgy puddings competing. You could enter something else—your gingerbread, maybe, or those lovely sugar cookies. Rose smiled insecurely. It would save everyone the embarrassment. . . "

Faye felt her jaw tighten. "I think I'll take my chances."

"Suit yourself." Rose turned toward the door accepting the rebuke, then paused. "Oh, and Arthur Whitford called the Historical Society this morning. He's been looking through some old documents and found something... interesting. He wants to discuss it at the Ball." She smiled that not-quite smile again. "Should be quite the evening."

After Rose left, Faye realized her hand had drifted to her pocket, where the scrap of paper with Lot 47 still rested.

"What was that about?" Tessa asked.

"I have no idea." Faye pulled out the paper, studied the jagged handwriting. Just a coincidence. "But something tells me this week is going to be more interesting than I planned."

Outside, snow began to fall in earnest, blanketing Butternut Cove in white. Through the window, Faye watched it transform the streets into a Christmas card scene—all twinkling lights and frosted windows and the kind of peace that makes you believe nothing bad could happen here.

She turned back to her figgy puddings, pushing down the unease that had settled in her chest.

I'm fine, she told herself again. *Everything is fine.*

But in Butternut Cove, ordinary never lasted long.

2

Secrets on the Cliffs
TUESDAY, DECEMBER 16TH.

After closing the café, Faye drove out to Tessa's cliffside bungalow with Tiny sprawled across the back seat. The Dane had a gift for making any vehicle feel smaller than it was.

The bungalow sat at the edge of the world, or so it seemed —perched on a bluff overlooking the Atlantic, far enough from town to feel like another planet. Faye loved the view but understood why Dixie had needed something more. Teenagers thrive on activity, on being in the center of things. Out here, the only company was the wind and the waves.

"Tea?" Tessa called from the kitchen as Faye let herself in.

"Please."

Faye sank into the overstuffed armchair by the picture window, the panoramic view of the ocean stretching endlessly before her. She studiously ignored the chaos of Tessa's living space—books stacked precariously, a half-knitted scarf draped over the couch, an empty teacup on the side table. Tessa had been twin Alan's messy wife, the one who operated on creative chaos while Faye kept everything in its place.

Tiny had already claimed his spot on the rug in front of the fireplace, limbs arranged with careless precision, his massive body radiating contentment and warmth.

"So," Tessa said, handing Faye a steaming cup and settling onto the couch. "How are you really doing? Yesterday was..."

"I'm fine." The words came automatically. "Busy. The Ball is in five days, and I've got a mountain of figgy pudding to make."

Tessa gave her that look—the one that said she wasn't buying it. "Faye. It was the anniversary. You're allowed to not be fine."

"I know." Faye wrapped her hands around the warm cup, staring out at the grey December sea. "But being not-fine doesn't change anything, does it? Derek and Jenny are still gone. Life goes on. The café needs me. Dixie needs stability. I can't afford to fall apart."

"No one's asking you to fall apart. I'm just asking you to feel something. Talk to someone. Me, if you want. Or—"

"I feel plenty," Faye said, more sharply than she intended. She softened her voice. "I just... process differently. You know that."

Tessa let it go, but the concern didn't leave her eyes. "Okay. But I'm here. Whenever you're ready."

Faye changed the subject. "How do you think Dixie is settling in at my place? Any problems?"

"Are you kidding? She texts me every day about how much she loves being in town. She's made friends with half the café regulars, she's joined some after-school thing at the library, and she's already talking about helping Callie with the Christmas rush at the bakery." Tessa smiled. "You've been good for her, Faye. Having her there has been good for both of you."

"She's good company." Faye sipped her tea. "And Tiny adores her. She sneaks him treats when she thinks I'm not looking."

The front door burst open bringing a gust of cold air and the girl herself, cheeks pink from the wind. Faye turned to Tessa, "Speaking of Dixie—"

"It's gorgeous out!" Dixie announced, stamping snow from her boots. "The sun came out and everything's sparkling. We should walk the cliffs before it gets dark!"

Tessa and Faye exchanged a glance.

"Fresh air might do us all good," Tessa said.

"Tiny could use the exercise," Faye agreed, though the Dane didn't look particularly enthusiastic about leaving his warm spot by the fire.

<hr />

BUNDLED IN COATS AND SCARVES, they walked the rugged path along the cliffs, the ocean crashing against the rocks below. Tiny plodded along beside Faye, his massive head level with her hip. He wasn't a dog who bounded or barked at seagulls—he simply accompanied, steady and calm, a living anchor.

The late afternoon light turned the water to hammered silver. In the distance, a sailboat cut across the horizon, its white sails catching the last of the sun.

"Look," Dixie said, pointing ahead. "Someone else had the same idea."

Two figures stood at the observation point, silhouettes against the pale sky. As they drew closer, Faye recognized them: Margaret Ellis, the town historian, and Beatrice Lark-spur, Arthur Whitford's spirited sister. Beatrice beamed at them. Arthur's sister had traded the Whitford name for her husband's forty years ago and Butternut Cove for San Francisco not long after, but she still had the family look—patrician nose, silver hair swept back elegantly. She came back every December, she'd told Faye once, because Christmas wasn't Christmas without snow and the smell of the sea.

"Margaret! Beatrice!" Faye called, waving.

Margaret turned, her face lighting up. She was in her early seventies, sharp-eyed and sharp-minded, the kind of woman who remembered every detail of every conversation. Her curls were spring-warm, cropped just below the ear, a salt-and-pepper silver that caught light like frost on pine—thick, lively, and unapologetically full of personality. "Faye! What a lovely surprise. And Tessa, Dixie—how wonderful."

Beatrice beamed at them. She had the Whitford look—but none of her brother Arthur's formality. Where Arthur was reserved and careful, Beatrice was warm and impulsive.

"We were just imagining sails on the horizon," Beatrice said, gesturing toward the sea. "Ships coming into harbor the way they did two hundred years ago."

"Beatrice has made a remarkable discovery," Margaret added, her eyes bright with scholarly excitement. "A map of the China trade routes that included Butternut Cove as a stopping point."

"The ships would moor at Beacon Hall's private dock," Beatrice explained, her voice animated. "It was a major transfer point for goods coming into Salem harbor. Tea, silk, porcelain—and according to some records, something more valuable that went missing during a ship's last visit."

Dixie's eyes went wide. "Missing? Like treasure?"

Beatrice leaned in conspiratorially. "The Whitford family has always whispered about hidden jewels. A fortune that was supposedly smuggled ashore and never recovered. Most people assume it's just a legend, but Margaret's been digging through the archives and..." She glanced at the historian.

Margaret's expression grew more guarded. "I've found

some... irregularities in the old records. Things that don't quite add up." She hesitated. "I'd rather not say more until I've had a chance to verify everything. But it's significant. Possibly very significant."

Faye felt a familiar tingle of curiosity. "What kind of irregularities?"

Margaret shook her head. "I really shouldn't speculate. But I'll say this—sometimes the secrets of the past have a way of echoing into the present." Her gaze drifted out to sea, troubled. "Butternut Cove has always had its mysteries. I'm beginning to think some of them never went away."

Before Faye could press further, Beatrice changed the subject.

"Speaking of mysteries—have you seen the lighthouse lately? The Shands have been restoring it. Quite the undertaking."

"I've driven past," Tessa said. "It's looking beautiful. They must have spent a fortune."

"What surprises me," Beatrice continued, "is how quickly they got approval. That land is part of the water preserve— the most difficult designation in the county. Arthur had a simple addition to his property questioned for months, but the Shands sailed through without a single objection." She frowned. "It struck me as odd."

Margaret and Beatrice exchanged a look that Faye couldn't quite read.

"Arthur's been looking into it," Margaret said quietly. "He thinks something isn't right with the land records. Property transfers that don't follow normal patterns."

"Is that what he wants to discuss at the Ball?" Faye asked, remembering Rose's cryptic comment from yesterday.

Margaret hesitated. "Perhaps. I'm not sure what he's planning to say publicly. But he's been... concerned."

A gust of wind swept across the cliffs, sharp and cold. In the distance, Faye noticed a figure standing near the tree line

—a man in a dark coat, watching them. Something about his posture seemed familiar.

She squinted against the light. Was that Peter Grayson?

But when she looked again, the figure was gone. Just a shadow among the pines.

"Getting cold," Tessa said, wrapping her arms around herself. "We should head back before we lose the light."

They said their goodbyes, Margaret promising to share more once she'd finished her research. Beatrice pressing them all to save some of the figgy pudding for her at the Ball.

As they walked back toward the bungalow, Dixie chattered about hidden treasure and secret jewels, Faye found herself thinking about Margaret's words.

Sometimes the secrets of the past have a way of echoing into the present.

She pulled her coat tighter against the wind, suddenly chilled in a way that had nothing to do with the December air.

⊂⊃

THAT EVENING, driving back to town with Tiny snoring softly in the back seat, Faye's phone buzzed with a text from Luke. She pulled to the side of the road.

Luke: Heard you were out at the cliffs today. Everything okay?

She smiled despite herself. Small towns. Nothing stayed private for long.

Faye: Fine. Just fresh air with Tessa and Dixie. Ran into Margaret and Beatrice.

A pause.

Luke: Margaret's been working on something. She seems worried. Keep an eye out?

Faye frowned at the screen. What did Luke know that he wasn't saying?

Faye: Worried about what?

But Luke didn't respond.

And by the time Faye pulled into her driveway on Ocean Street, the question had lodged itself in her mind like a splinter.

Dixie was already home—Tessa had dropped her off—and the lights in the kitchen glowed warmly through the windows. Faye could see her niece's silhouette moving around, probably starting dinner.

Home. Family. The ordinary rhythms of life.

But as she climbed out of the Jeep, Faye couldn't shake the feeling that something was shifting beneath the surface of Butternut Cove. Something that had been buried for a long time was beginning to stir.

She thought of Margaret's guarded expression. Beatrice's questions about the lighthouse. The figure watching from the tree line.

And Lot 47, scrawled on that scrap of paper she'd found on the cliffs.

It's nothing, she told herself, letting Tiny out of the car. *Just small-town gossip and old legends.*

But she didn't quite believe it.

Four days until the Victorian Ball. Four days until Arthur Whitford would say whatever he'd been planning to say.

Family Ties
WEDNESDAY, DECEMBER 17TH.
THREE DAYS UNTIL THE BALL.

After closing the café, Faye found herself surrounded by flour and sugar in her Victorian kitchen at 22 Ocean Street. This was the other side of Faye—the homebody, the baker, the woman who found peace in the precise measurements of a recipe.

Tiny lay sprawled across the kitchen sofa. His tail thumped lazily whenever Faye passed by him, which was often.

"You're a handsome boy," she told him affectionately. "A very large, very well-placed hazard."

From upstairs came the thump of music—Dixie working on homework, or more likely avoiding it. The house had felt different since her niece moved in three months ago. Fuller. Livelier. Less like a museum of grief and more like a home.

Not that Faye would admit how much she needed the company.

She was piping icing onto sugar cookies—stars and snowflakes and little Christmas trees—when the doorbell rang. Tiny lifted his head but didn't bother getting up. Some guard dog.

"I'll get it!" Dixie's voice rang from upstairs, followed by the thunder of feet on the stairs.

"Dixie, you don't have to—" But her niece was already at the door.

"Detective Luke! Hey!" Dixie's voice carried easily to the kitchen. "Aunt Faye's making cookies. Want one? They're amazing."

Faye wiped her hands on her apron, suddenly aware of the flour dusted across her sweater and probably her face. She resisted the urge to check her reflection in the a row of copper pots polished to a comforting glow that hung above the prep counter.

Luke appeared in the kitchen doorway, Dixie chattering beside him. He wore his usual leather jacket, snow melting in his dark hair, and his eyes crinkled when he saw her.

"Looks like I interrupted a crime scene," he said, surveying the flour-dusted counters. "Death by sugar cookie?"

"Very funny." Faye gestured to a stool at the island. "Sit. I'll make you some chai. Unless this is an official visit?"

"Semi-official." Luke settled onto the stool, reaching down to scratch Tiny behind the ears. The Dane's tail thumped approval. "I wanted to follow up on something. And maybe steal a cookie."

"Dixie, would you take Tiny out back for a few minutes?" Faye asked.

Her niece's eyes lit up with curiosity, but she knew better than to argue. "Come on, big guy." She snapped her fingers and Tiny heaved himself up with a dramatic sigh, following her to the back door.

Once they were alone, Faye set a cup of chai in front of Luke and leaned against the counter. "Semi-official?"

Luke wrapped his hands around the warm cup. "Margaret Ellis. You saw her yesterday at the cliffs."

"I did. She seemed... preoccupied. She mentioned finding irregularities in some old records."

"Did she say what kind of irregularities?"

"No. She was being careful about it. Said she didn't want to speculate until she'd verified everything." Faye studied Luke's face. "Why? Is something wrong?"

Luke hesitated—a tell she'd learned to recognize. He was deciding how much to share.

"Margaret came to the station yesterday afternoon," he said finally. "Wanted to file some kind of preliminary report about irregularities in property records. Said she had concerns about recent land transfers in Butternut Cove."

"Property records?" Faye thought of Beatrice's comment about the lighthouse approval. "Did she name anyone specific?"

"She was going to bring documentation today. More complete evidence." Luke's jaw tightened. "She didn't show."

"Maybe she's still gathering it."

"Maybe." Luke didn't sound convinced. "I called Beacon Hall. Henry said she's been in the archives all day, won't take calls. Arthur's worried about her—says she's been acting strangely for weeks."

Faye felt a flutter of unease. "You think something's wrong?"

"I think she's scared of something. Or someone." Luke met her eyes. "And I think you should be careful. Whatever she's found, it's got her rattled. I don't want you getting caught up in it."

"I'm just baking cookies, Luke."

"You're also on the Beacon Hall Board nomination list. And you're the kind of person who asks questions." He softened. "I'm not trying to scare you. I'm just... looking out for you."

Something warm flickered in Faye's chest, and she quickly tamped it down. "I appreciate that. But I'm fine."

There was that word again. Fine. Her universal deflection.

Luke seemed to recognize it too. He changed the subject. "On a completely different note—have you talked to my cousin Peter lately?"

"Peter? He was in the café Monday. Bought his usual cookies." Faye frowned. "Why?"

"He's been asking around about property records too. Old deeds, survey maps, transfer documents." Luke's tone was carefully neutral. "Says it's for his antique appraisal work, but..."

"But?"

"But Peter's never been interested in land history before. His specialty is furniture and decorative arts." Luke shrugged. "It's probably nothing. He's had some family troubles lately—legal issues. Maybe he's looking to diversify his business."

"Legal issues?"

"Old family stuff. Lawsuits from years ago that are still dragging on. It's complicated." Luke waved a hand dismissively, but something in his expression suggested he was choosing his words carefully. "Anyway. Just thought it was interesting that he and Margaret are both suddenly fascinated by the same subject."

Faye filed that away. Peter Grayson and property records. Margaret's research. The lighthouse approval. Arthur's concerns. "Actually," Dean said slowly, "I remember the Grayson's. Peter's father, Edward—he was a character. Charming as anything, but everyone knew he had a gambling problem. Lost the family fortune at the card tables, or so the story went. By the time he died, there was nothing left but debts and that dusty shop." He shrugged. "Always wondered how Peter managed to turn things around."

Threads. They felt like threads of something, but she couldn't see the pattern yet.

The back door opened and Dixie tumbled in with Tiny, both of them bringing the cold with them.

"It's freezing out there!" Dixie announced, rubbing her hands together. "I think it's going to snow again tonight."

"Perfect weather for decorating the Christmas tree," Faye said, grateful for the interruption. The conversation with Luke had left her unsettled in ways she didn't want to examine. "Luke, would you like to stay for dinner? We're trimming the tree tonight."

"Please say yes!" Dixie bounced on her toes. "Aunt Faye makes amazing pot roast, and we have enough ornaments to cover three trees."

Luke's eyes met Faye's for a moment longer than necessary. "I appreciate the offer, but I've got to get back to the station. Paperwork doesn't do itself."

"Another time, then," Faye said, surprised by her own disappointment.

"Another time." He stood, grabbing a sugar cookie from the cooling rack. "For the road."

Faye walked him to the door. On the porch, he paused.

"Faye. What I said about being careful—I meant it. Something's going on in this town. I can feel it." His voice dropped. "And if you hear anything, or see anything that seems off... you'll tell me won't you?"

"Of course." She forced a smile. "I'm just a café owner, Luke. What could I possibly stumble into?"

His expression said he didn't buy that for a second. "Right. Just a café owner. With a talent for asking questions and a habit of being in the wrong place at the wrong time."

"That was one time."

"Twice. At least."

She laughed despite herself, and something shifted in the air between them—a warmth that had nothing to do with the chai. Luke seemed to feel it too. He stepped back.

"Good night, Faye. Enjoy the tree trimming."

"Good night, Luke."

She watched him walk to his truck, the snow crunching under his boots. He waved once before climbing in, and then he was gone, taillights disappearing into the December night.

———

LATER THAT EVENING, with Tessa arrived for dinner and the pot roast warming the house with its rich aroma, Faye stood back to admire their work.

The Christmas tree glowed in the bay window, laden with ornaments collected over generations. Glass balls from her grandmother. Wooden figures Derek had carved during their first winter together. A tiny angel Jenny had made in kindergarten, lopsided and perfect. Faye touched the lopsided angel, remembering small fingers sticky with glue, a proud gap-toothed smile.

Faye's throat tightened. She turned away before Tessa or Dixie could notice.

"It's beautiful," Dixie breathed, her face lit by the colored lights. "Best tree ever."

"It really is," Tessa agreed, wrapping an arm around her daughter. Her eyes found Faye's across the room, full of gentle understanding.

Faye managed a smile. "Who wants hot cocoa?"

In the kitchen, alone for a moment, she let herself feel it— the weight of all those memories hanging on the tree. Derek and Jenny, present but absent. The ache of loving people who weren't here to love back.

Tiny pressed against her leg, his massive head level with her hip. He always knew.

"I'm fine," she whispered, though no one had asked. "I'm fine."

But standing in her kitchen on a December evening, with laughter drifting in from the living room and grief lodged like a stone in her chest, Faye wondered how long she could keep saying that before it stopped being true.

Or before she finally admitted it never had been.

4

Things Are Not
What They Seem

THURSDAY, DECEMBER 18TH.
TWO DAYS UNTIL THE BALL.

The morning rush at *The Heirloom Table Café* was in full swing when the door chimed and Arthur Whitford stepped inside, followed by his assistant Henry Lawson. A ripple of warmth passed through the café—Arthur had that effect on people. He was old Butternut Cove, fourth generation, the kind of man who remembered everyone's name and never failed to ask after their families.

"Good morning, good morning!" Arthur called out, his voice carrying the boom of someone accustomed to addressing crowds. He wore a camel overcoat and a tartan scarf, his silver hair swept back from a patrician face lined with smile creases. "Merry Christmas to all!"

Christmas carols played softly from the speakers—*God Rest*

Ye Merry Gentlemen—and the aroma of cinnamon and cloves hung warm in the air. A chorus of greetings answered Arthur. Mabel Thornton waved from her corner table, a white bakery box beside her tea. Ivy Chen raised her coffee cup in salute, another *Heirloom Table Cafe* box at her elbow—a gift for someone, no doubt. Even old Mr. Plum, who rarely acknowledged anyone before his second cup, managed a nod.

Henry Lawson hovered a step behind Arthur, as he always did—quiet, watchful, utterly devoted. He'd been Arthur's assistant for nearly twenty years, ever since Arthur had taken over stewardship of Beacon Hall. As Arthur worked the room, Henry's gaze drifted toward the door, and when it opened to admit a delivery driver, his shoulders dropped slightly. Not who he was looking for.

"Henry, would you pick up my usual order?" Arthur called over his shoulder. "And see if Margaret Ellis has been in this morning. I have some documents she requested."

Something flickered across Henry's face at Margaret's name—hope, perhaps, or longing—gone so quickly Faye might have imagined it. "Of course, Mr. Whitford." He moved to the counter, his voice softening. "Has Margaret—Miss Ellis—been in today?"

"Not yet," Faye said, boxing up an assortment of ginger snaps and snickerdoodles. "But she usually comes by in the afternoon."

Henry nodded, accepting the box with both hands, almost reverently. "I'll let Mr. Whitford know."

Faye emerged from behind the counter as Arthur finished his rounds. "Arthur! What brings you in?"

"Christmas spirit, my dear. Pure Christmas spirit." Arthur clasped her hands in both of his, his blue eyes twinkling. "And I wanted to thank you personally for all your work on the Ball preparations. Tessa tells me the decorations are going to be magnificent."

"We're doing our best." Faye smiled.

"Your best is always exceptional." Arthur's expression shifted slightly—a flicker of something beneath the bonhomie. "I'm looking forward to our conversation on Saturday. Before the Ball. There are things I'd like to discuss with you. Important things."

"Your earlier voicemail surprised me, Arthur. You mentioned my family's history with the Whitfords."

Arthur glanced around the crowded café, then lowered his voice. "Not here. But yes. I've discovered something in the archives that concerns both our families. Something that's been buried for a very long time." He squeezed her hands. "Saturday. We'll talk then."

Before Faye could press further, Arthur had released her hands and was moving through the café, shaking hands, spreading Christmas cheer like a politician on the campaign trail. Henry followed silently, the bakery box tucked under his arm, offering polite nods to those Arthur greeted.

At the door, Arthur turned back and caught Faye's eye. He raised a hand in farewell.

"See you soon," he called.

Then he was gone, Henry close behind, and the café settled back into its usual rhythms. But Faye couldn't shake the feeling that something had been left unsaid. Something important.

▭

LATER THAT MORNING, Tessa appeared at the café with a mission.

"I need to pick up the cake topper from Kent Blake's shop," she announced. "For the gingerbread house centerpiece at the Ball. Come with me? I could use the moral support."

"Moral support for picking up a cake topper?" Faye joked.

"Moral support for dealing with Kent Blake." Tessa made a face. "You know how he gets."

Faye did know. Kent Blake ran Butternut Cove's premier wedding cake shop, *Simply I Do*, with the attitude of someone who believed he should be decorating cakes for royalty instead of coastal New England townspeople. His talent was undeniable. His personality was... an acquired taste.

"Let me get Tiny, he could use the walk." Faye said.

Getting Tiny ready for a December walk was no small undertaking. The Dane stood with an expression of profound suffering as Faye buckled him into a red tartan Christmas coat that matched the ribbon on his collar. The pièce de résistance was a knitted hat with ear holes—green with a pompom—that Dixie had bought at the craft fair last weekend.

"He looks ridiculous," Tessa observed.

"He looks festive," Faye corrected. "And warm. He hates the cold."

Tiny's expression suggested he hated the outfit more, but he allowed himself to be led outside with only a single, deeply aggrieved sigh.

They walked through town, past the harbor where fishing boats bobbed in the grey water, their masts strung with Christmas lights that would twinkle to life at dusk. Past the bookshop with its window display of Christmas mysteries, past the gorgeous balsam wreaths that hung on every door—Celia Shand's handiwork, each one a unique arrangement of balls, bells, ribbons, and angels. The Shands had only been in Butternut Cove a few years, but Celia had already made herself indispensable to the town's Christmas traditions. Faye turned to catch the sound of the church bell chime, and from an open doorway came the sound of children singing *Deck the Halls*. She turned to Tessa, the children's voices sound so sweet.

Halfway down Harbor Street, a van pulled up to the curb —Evan Doyle, Yves's nephew, making deliveries for his uncle's

Lobsta Shack restaurant. He waved cheerfully as he hopped out, and Faye noticed a familiar white box on the passenger seat. One of hers. Half the town seemed to be exchanging her cookies as Christmas gifts this week.

Kent Blake's shop occupied a prime corner location with large windows showcasing elaborate wedding cakes and seasonal displays. Today's window featured a five-tier master-piece decorated with sugar snowflakes and edible silver leaf, surrounded by porcelain angels and flickering electric candles.

"You wait here," Faye told Tiny, looping his leash around the bench outside. "We'll be quick."

Tiny sat down heavily, his Christmas coat bunching around his shoulders, the ridiculous pompom hat Faye had insisted on perching crookedly between his ears. He fixed her with a look of absolute betrayal.

"Five minutes," Faye promised.

Tiny was unconvinced.

Inside, the shop smelled of vanilla and fondant, warm and sweet against the December chill. Glass cases displayed minia-ture wedding cakes, elaborate petit fours, and sugar flowers so realistic they seemed ready to bloom. A small Christmas tree stood in the corner, decorated entirely with edible ornaments.

Kent Blake stood behind the counter, deep in conversation with two women. Faye recognized them both immediately—Rose Fairweather, an associate archivist at Beacon Hall, and Charlotte Whitford, Arthur's niece.

Rose turned at the sound of the door. As always, she was dressed as if she'd stepped out of a fashion magazine rather than a small coastal town—today in head-to-toe Burberry, her dark hair swept into an artful chignon, gold jewelry catching the light. While her appearance seemed out of place in Butternut Cover, it also inspired admiration.

"Faye! Tessa!" Rose's smile was bright but brief. "We were just leaving."

Charlotte Whitford offered a polite nod but didn't speak.

She was impeccably dressed in cream cashmere and pearls, her blonde hair smooth and perfect, her posture that of someone who'd attended the right schools and belonged to the right clubs. She had Arthur's blue eyes, but where his were warm, hers were cool—assessing. She held one of Kent's signature gold boxes, but Faye noticed a smaller white box tucked under her arm as well. Heirloom Table packaging.

"Charlotte, have you met Faye Harper?" Rose asked. "She owns *The Heirloom Table Café*. Her figgy pudding is the one to beat at the Ball."

"Charmed." Charlotte's voice was pleasant but distant. Then something shifted in her expression. "Rose mentioned that Margaret Ellis has been spending quite a bit of time at your café lately. Doing research, she said."

"Margaret comes in most afternoons," Faye said carefully. "She likes the quiet."

"Margaret does love her research." Charlotte's smiled. "Always digging into the past. Some things are better left buried, don't you think? Old history. Old... indiscretions." She adjusted her gloves with precise, controlled movements. "But Margaret never could resist a secret."

Rose shifted uncomfortably, and Faye caught her glancing between Charlotte and the door. Whatever this tension was about, Rose knew something.

"We really must go," Charlotte said, her composure restored. "Oliver's waiting."

"Of course." Rose air-kissed in Faye's general direction, her relief palpable. "See you Saturday!"

They swept out, leaving a cloud of expensive perfume in their wake. Through the window, Faye watched them approach a car parked at the curb—and what a car it was. A Bentley Continental, 2025 model, in a color she'd later learn was called Sequin Blue. It gleamed like liquid metal in the grey December light, absurdly beautiful, utterly out of place on the cobblestone streets of Butternut Cove.

A man stepped out from the driver's side—Oliver Ashworth, presumably. Charlotte's husband. Dark hair, strong jaw, the kind of profile that belonged on currency. He opened the rear door for Rose, then moved to the passenger side for Charlotte, his movements precise and courteous.

Faye noticed several white bakery boxes stacked on the back seat. Her boxes. Oliver caught her looking through the window and held her gaze for a moment—something unreadable in his expression.

"Generous gifts," he said, his voice carrying over the Bentley and through the briefly open door. "They smooth over so many... complications."

Then Charlotte slid into the passenger seat, Rose was already in back, and the Bentley pulled away, silent as a whisper.

"Some people," Kent Blake said, and Faye couldn't tell if his tone was admiring or disdainful. Possibly both.

She turned to face him. Kent was a tall man in his fifties, handsome in a faded way, with silver-streaked hair and the perpetually dissatisfied expression of someone who believed the world had failed to appreciate his genius. He held a white Heirloom Table box of his own—collecting them like everyone else in town, apparently.

"Faye Harper," he said, drawing out her name. "Come to check on the competition?"

"We're here for the cake topper," Tessa interjected. "For the gingerbread centerpiece."

"Ah yes. The gingerbread house." Kent's lips curved into something not quite a smile. "A charming tradition. Though I must say, I'm rather looking forward to Saturday's dessert competition. My figgy pudding is exceptional this year. *Exceptional.*"

"I'm sure it is," Faye said evenly.

He continued "I've been perfecting the my recipe for

months. A touch of saffron in the custard, aged brandy, figs sourced from a specific orchard in Portugal."

He leaned forward conspiratorially. "Between you and me, Arthur owes me a favor or two. We go back years, Arthur and I. He knows quality when he sees it."

There was something beneath the boast—an edge. Faye remembered hearing that Kent had once applied for a position with the Historical Society, years ago. Arthur had turned him down. Ancient history, but Kent didn't seem the type to forget a slight.

"May the best pudding win," Faye said, keeping her voice pleasant.

Kent studied her for a moment, then turned to retrieve a box from behind the counter. "Your topper. One Victorian manor in spun sugar and gold leaf. My finest work, if I do say so myself."

Tessa paid while Faye glanced out the window. Tiny sat exactly where they'd left him, pompom hat now completely askew, radiating the kind of dignified misery only a Dane in a Christmas costume could achieve. A small crowd of tourists had gathered to take photos.

"Your dog is going viral," Kent observed drily.

Faye smiled despite herself. "He does have a certain presence."

———

BACK AT THE CAFÉ, Faye found Callie Sweet waiting with her daily bread delivery, Jaxson at her feet and Fig surveying the room from her shoulder carrier with regal disdain.

"There you are!" Callie set the basket on the counter. The warm scent of fresh-baked bread mingled with the café's cinnamon and pine. "I was starting to think you'd abandoned ship."

"Reconnaissance mission to enemy territory," Tessa said, holding up the cake topper box.

"Kent Blake's?" Callie made a face. "How is our favorite humble artisan?"

"Confident. Very confident." Faye unclipped Tiny's leash, removed the hated pompom hat and his tartan coat—draping the later over the back of a chair. She watched the Dane make a beeline for his spot near the fireplace. He'd earned a rest.

"Well, confidence doesn't win competitions. Talent does." Callie grinned. "And you've got plenty of that. How's the pudding coming?"

"Third batch is setting now. I think this one might be the winner."

They chatted about the Ball preparations, about Callie's new assistant Allison who was still finding her footing. "She's willing, bless her," Callie said with a sigh, "but she's more comfortable with horses than with pastry. I've got her doing deliveries and bookkeeping for now. She'll be helping serve at the Ball, though—I need all hands on deck."

"How did she end up in Butternut Cove?" Tessa asked.

"Someone she met at the regatta told her about it. She needed a fresh start—divorce, I think, though she doesn't talk about it much. Only twenty-five and starting over." Callie shook her head. "This town has a way of collecting people who need a soft place to land."

Faye thought about that. She'd been one of those people once. Still was, maybe.

It was nearly noon when Callie glanced at the clock and gasped. "I've got to run. Allison's still nervous about handling the lunch rush alone." She gathered Jaxson's leash and adjusted Fig's carrier. "See you both Saturday. And don't let Kent Blake rattle you!"

AFTER CALLIE LEFT, Faye returned to her pudding. She was brushing brandy onto the finished surface—watching it gleam in the afternoon light—when movement outside the window caught her eye.

Noel's delivery van was parked across the street. Strange— he'd told her he was leaving for Vermont on Monday, wouldn't be back until the 26th. Yet there he was, loading boxes into the back. Not just her boxes, she noticed. He had packages from several shops—Kent's gold boxes, something from the florist, brown paper parcels from the general store.

As she watched, three different people approached him in quick succession. Rose Fairweather handed him an envelope. Peter Grayson—Luke's look alike cousin, passed him a small package wrapped in brown paper. And finally, Kent Blake approached with one of his gold boxes, exchanging a few words before Noel added it to his haul.

Noel climbed into the van, started the engine, and pulled away from the curb. Faye watched him turn onto Harbor Road, heading... somewhere.

Half the town seemed to be using him for last-minute Christmas deliveries. Perfectly normal.

She returned to her pudding.

<hr>

AS THE CAFÉ wound down for the afternoon, Faye noticed the snowfall had intensified outside, dimming the light filtering through the windows. Christmas lights twinkled on the store- fronts across the street, and someone had started a fire in the pot belly stove at the bookshop next door—she could smell woodsmoke mingling with the scent of her baking. Tiny lay sprawled by the radiator, taking up an improbable amount of floor space.

A voice called her name from the corner table.

"Excuse me, Faye?"

It was Yves Brown, owner of the Lobsta Shack, holding a cup of steaming chai. He was a weathered man in his sixties, quiet and observant, the kind of person who noticed things others missed.

Faye approached his table. "Everything okay with your chai, Yves? I saw your nephew earlier today delivering gifts from the sea."

"The chai is perfect. Evan is a good young man." He glanced around, ensuring no one was listening, then lowered his voice. "I overheard something today. I think you should know."

Faye had started to leave but turned back, "What is it?"

"I was at the post office this morning. Arthur Whitford was there, having what I can only describe as a heated conversation on his phone. He kept saying 'I won't be silenced' and 'the town deserves to know.'" Yves paused. "He looked concerned. And angry. I've never seen Arthur like that."

A chill ran down Faye's spine.

"Did you hear who he was talking to?"

"No. But afterward, I saw him walk over to Peter Grayson's antique shop. They spoke on the sidewalk for several minutes. Arthur was gesturing—pointing toward the harbor, toward Beacon Hall. Peter just stood there with his arms crossed, very still." Yves met her eyes. "I know you are going to the Ball. But I wanted you to be aware that things are not what they seem in Butternut Cove."

Before Faye could respond, her cell phone vibrated in her apron pocket.

"Excuse me." She stepped away and pulled out the phone. It was the timer for her figgy pudding, she needed to baste it again

‌⸻

SHE WAS ABOUT to lock the door and turn the sign to closed.

When Margaret Ellis stepped in, looking nothing like her usual composed self. Her curly silver hair was disheveled. Her coat was buttoned wrong. And her eyes—her sharp, scholar's eyes—darted around the café as if expecting to find someone watching.

"Margaret?" Faye asked. "Are you all right?"

"Fine. I'm fine." Margaret's hands were shaking. "I just—I needed to—" She stopped, took a breath. "Do you have a moment? Somewhere private?"

"Of course." Faye led her to her office behind the kitchen, closing the door. "What's wrong?"

Margaret sank into the wing chair by the desk, her composure crumbling. "I've made a terrible mistake. I've been researching—the land records, the property transfers—and I found something. Something that explains everything. The lighthouse approval. The harbor lots. The way certain families have been quietly buying up Butternut Cove."

"Margaret, slow down. What did you find?"

"I can't—" She shook her head. "I can't tell you yet. I need to verify everything first. I need to be certain before I accuse anyone." She reached into her bag and pressed a small notebook into Faye's hands. "But if something happens to me—"

"Margaret!" Faye's voice sharpened. "What do you mean, *if something happens?*"

"I'm being watched. I'm sure of it." Margaret's eyes filled with tears. "I went to the police yesterday, but they don't understand. They think I'm an old woman seeing shadows." She gripped Faye's arm. "Keep this safe. Don't tell anyone you have it. And if I don't come to the Ball on Saturday—"

"You're scaring me."

"Good." Margaret stood abruptly. "You should be scared. We all should be." She moved toward the door, then paused.

"I left something else for you. In your cookbook—the one on the shelf by the register. I slipped a note inside yesterday. Read it. And be careful who you trust."

Before Faye could respond, Margaret was gone, the café door swinging shut behind her.

Faye went back to her office, closed the door and stood frozen, the notebook heavy in her hands. She flipped it open to a random page: columns of names, dates, property descriptions. Margaret's handwriting was cramped and hurried in places, the letters bleeding into each other. Nothing that made immediate sense—a scholar's shorthand, meaningful only to its author.

Her phone buzzed. A text from Arthur:

Please come to Beacon Hall this afternoon. 4 P.M.
There's been a development. Come alone.
Faye checked the time. 3:15 P.M.

OUTSIDE, snow drifted lazily through the December air—more suggestion than storm, the way it always was this close to the ocean. Christmas lights glowed in shop windows, and she could hear bells somewhere—church bells, or perhaps the Salvation Army collector on the corner.

Tiny lifted his head from his spot by the fireplace, watching Faye with dark, knowing eyes. His tail thumped once against the floor—a question.

"Yes, you're coming." Faye grabbed her coat and Tiny's leash.

The Dane rose with the slow dignity of someone who'd been expecting this all along. He stretched his long legs before padding to Faye's side.

"We'll be back soon," Faye called to Tessa, who was closing out the register.

But even as she clipped the leash to Tiny's collar, she wondered if that was true.

5

The Archives

THURSDAY, DECEMBER
18TH - LATE AFTERNOON

The late afternoon sun cast long shadows across Ocean Street as Faye pulled her Jeep into the gravel lot behind Beacon Hall. She checked the clock on her dashboard: 3:47 P.M.

Thirteen minutes early. As usual.

She'd never been able to break the habit, despite years of teasing from friends, like dear Tessa, who ran perpetually late. But Arthur wouldn't mind. He was as punctual as she was, and his text had seemed urgent.

She pulled out her phone and read it again:

Please come to Beacon Hall this afternoon. 4 P.M.
There's been a development. Come alone.

The message had arrived at 3:15 P.M., while she was doing additional basting of the most recent figgy pudding experiment. She'd barely had time to wash her hands and change out of her flour-dusted apron before heading over. Arthur hadn't said what the "development" was, but she assumed it had something to do with his great grandmother, Alice Whitford's recipe collection—perhaps he'd found more documents for her to examine.

"Come alone" was a bit odd, but Arthur was nothing if not particular about privacy. Perhaps he wanted to discuss something sensitive before involving others.

Tiny sat alert in the back seat, his massive Dane head leaning on Faye's shoulder. She reached up and scratched behind the dog's ears.

"Ready for another adventure, honey?"

Tiny's tail thumped against the seat. He'd been Faye's constant companion since the accident, trained to sense the onset of her panic attacks before she recognized them herself. Five years later, she still needed him—though the episodes came less frequently now. Butternut Cove had been good for Faye.

She clipped Tiny's service vest into place.

Tiny had been trained as a psychiatric service dog after the accident—not for flashy commands, just for steadiness when she needed it most.

They crossed the parking lot together, her boots crunching on the frost-tipped gravel. Beacon Hall rose before them, its Victorian grandeur softened by the Christmas wreaths adorning every window. Candles flickered in the lower rooms, and somewhere inside, she could hear the faint strains of carol music.

The front door stood slightly ajar.

Faye paused, her hand hovering over the brass knocker. That was unusual. Arthur was meticulous about security, especially with the historical society's artifacts stored inside. This time of year, with Beacon Hall running on limited winter hours, the building should have been staffed at the entrance or locked up entirely.

Maybe he left it open because he's expecting me, she guessed.

But she was early. Arthur wouldn't have unlocked it yet.

She pushed the door open and stepped into the grand foyer.

"Hello? Arthur?"

Her voice echoed against the marble floors and wood-paneled walls. The Christmas tree in the corner sparkled with Victorian ornaments—glass baubles, tinsel garlands, hand-painted angels—but the room felt oddly hollow. No footsteps answered her call. No cheerful greeting from Henry, Arthur's ever-present assistant.

Where is everyone, she wondered.

Tiny pressed against her leg, a low whine building in his throat.

"What is it, honey?"

The Dane pulled toward the east corridor, where the archives were housed. Faye had spent many pleasant hours in that room, poring over Alice Whitford's recipe collection and the founding families' documents. Margaret Ellis practically lived there, cataloging and cross-referencing with the dedication of a scholar.

Margaret. Perhaps she was working late and could point Faye toward Arthur.

"Margaret?" Faye called as she followed Tiny down the corridor. "Are you here?"

Silence. But as they moved deeper into the east wing, Faye caught a faint scent of cedar and old paper, typical of the archives. Something unpleasant. Something that reminded her of chemistry class, of warnings about compounds you should never touch or taste.

Faint but unmistakable. The bitter fragrance of almonds.

Her steps slowed. Her heart began to pound.

The archives door was open, warm lamplight spilling into the hallway. Faye felt a flutter of relief—someone was here after all. But Tiny had stopped at the threshold, his body rigid, ears flat against his head. He wouldn't cross into the room.

"Tiny? What—"

She stepped past him and the word died in her throat.

THE ARCHIVES WERE IN CHAOS.

File drawers stood open, their contents scattered across the floor. Land records, property maps, yellowed documents that should have been handled with cotton gloves—all of it strewn about as if a storm had torn through the room. The reading lamp had been knocked over, casting harsh shadows across the walls. Daylight was dimming.

Margaret lay beside the oak reading table, a toppled stack of archive folders scattered near her. Her short, bouncy curls —silver-grey with a hint of soft wave—still framed her face as if she'd merely paused mid-thought, mid-project, mid-Christmas. One glove-clad hand rested palm-up on the Persian rug, her fingers gently arched, like the shape of a question left unanswered. There was no reflection now in those usual bright, intent eyes. No spark. Just the quiet left behind when the town's most tenacious historian stopped moving.

For a moment, Faye froze. Couldn't breathe. The room tilted, and she felt the familiar tightening in her chest, the world narrowing to a dark tunnel.

No. Not now.

Tiny was there instantly, pressing his solid weight against Faye's legs, grounding her licking her fingers and her hand. She responded and touched the dogs head feeling the warmth of his fur beneath her fingers, and forcing herself to breathe.

In through the nose. Out through the mouth. The way her therapist had taught her.

The tunnel receded. The room steadied.

"Good boy," she whispered, her voice shaking. "Good boy."

She knelt beside Margaret, though she already knew what she would find. The historian's skin was cool to the touch, her lips tinged with an unnatural blue. And there—beside her outstretched hand—sat a small bakery box from *The Heirloom Table Café*. Faye's own logo smiled up at her from the cardboard box. Inside, a single cookie lay with one bite missing.

Faye's stomach lurched. She hadn't sent Margaret any cookies. She hadn't sent anyone cookies today.

The bitter almond scent hung heavier here, unmistakable now. This wasn't a heart attack. This wasn't natural causes.

Someone had poisoned Margaret Ellis with a cookie bearing Faye's name.

She scrambled backward, her heart hammering.

How did my box get here?

The question cut through her panic like a blade. She tried to reason. She'd been at the café all day, well almost all day. She hadn't made deliveries. Yet here was her packaging, her logo, her…

She stopped.

My boxes are everywhere. I've seen them everywhere.

The realization hit her like cold water. She'd spent the past week packaging Christmas orders. Charlotte and Oliver had left Kent's shop carrying at least three of her boxes. Rose had picked up an order for the Historical Society volunteers. Even Kent Blake had bought cookies for his staff. Half the town had her boxes.

Anyone could have used one.

But someone had. Someone had taken her packaging—trusted, familiar, ubiquitous—and turned it into a murder weapon.

"Help!" The word tore like a shrill from her throat. "Someone help!"

Footsteps thundered down the corridor. Henry Lawson appeared first, his face draining of color as he took in the scene. Behind him came Rose Fairweather, her hand flying to her mouth.

"Dear God," Henry breathed. He rushed to Margaret's side, dropping to his knees. "Margaret. Margaret!" His voice cracked as he reached for her hand, then pulled back as if burned. "She's—she's—"

"Don't touch anything," Faye said, surprised by the steadiness of her own voice. "We need to call the police. Now."

Rose stood frozen in the doorway, her face a mask of shock. "I just saw her this morning. She was fine. She was working on something—said she'd found something important in the land records."

Land records.

Faye's gaze swept the scattered papers again. Property deeds. Survey maps. Transfer documents with dates going back decades—and some that looked far more recent. Margaret had been researching something, and whatever she'd found had gotten her killed.

Heavy footsteps echoed from the foyer, followed by a voice that made Faye's heart simultaneously sink and lift.

"Henry texted me—said the front door was open. What's going on? Is everything."

Arthur Whitford appeared in the doorway, still wearing his overcoat, snowflakes melting in his silver hair. He must have just arrived. His gaze swept the room—the scattered papers, the overturned lamp—and then found Margaret's body.

His face crumpled.

"No." The word came out as a moan. "No, no, no."

He staggered forward, and Henry caught him by the arm. "Mr. Whitford—Arthur—you shouldn't."

"She was my friend." Arthur's voice broke. "Fifty years. We've known each other fifty years." He sagged against Henry, then straightened, grief hardening into something else. His eyes found Faye. "What are you doing here?"

"You texted me. You said to come at four—that there had been a development."

Arthur stared at her. "I didn't send you any text."

The words landed like stones in still water. Faye felt the floor shift beneath her.

"But—I have it right here." She pulled out her phone, scrolling to the message. "See? It came from your number. 3:15 P.M. this afternoon."

Arthur took the phone, his hands trembling. He stared at the screen for a long moment, then shook his head slowly. "This isn't—I didn't write this. I was in a meeting with the mayor until 3:45 P.M. Ask anyone at Town Hall." He looked up at her, bewildered. "I don't understand. Why would someone send you a message pretending to be me?"

Rose made a small sound—something between a gasp and a cough. When Faye glanced at her, she was very pale, her hand pressed to her throat.

"That's—that's very strange," Rose said. Her voice was higher than usual. "Who would do something like that?"

Henry was frowning at Arthur's coat pocket. "Sir, do you have your phone?"

Arthur patted his pockets, then pulled out his cell phone. "It's right here. It's been with me all." He stopped, staring at the screen. "That's odd. There's an outgoing message I don't remember sending."

Faye's forced herself to think clearly. Someone had used Arthur's phone—or made it look like they had. Someone who wanted me at Beacon Hall at four o'clock. Someone who wanted me to find Margaret's body.

Someone who wanted me to look guilty.

The realization should have frightened her. Instead, she felt a flicker of something unexpected: resolve. Whoever had done this had gone to considerable trouble to make her look like a murderer. They'd stolen her bakery boxes, poisoned a kind old woman, and dragged her into the middle of it.

Well, she thought determinedly, they picked the wrong baker to frame.

"This isn't your fault," she said quietly to Arthur. "Margaret died because she found the truth. That's on whoever killed her."

She pulled out her phone with trembling fingers. "I'm calling Detective Grayson."

———

THE NEXT HOUR passed in a blur. Luke arrived with two officers, his face grim as he surveyed the scene. He took preliminary statements from everyone present, his eyes lingering on Faye when she described finding the bakery box and naming what she thought was the cyanide poisoning. He didn't say anything, but she saw the concern flicker across his face.

"The medical examiner will need to confirm the cause of death," Luke said quietly. But Faye continued. The blue discoloration, the bitter almond scent—it's consistent with poisoning.

Then Luke in an effort to calm her says, "We'll know more after the autopsy. Could be twenty-four to forty-eight hours before we get definitive results."

Faye nodded. She'd suspected as much. The bitter almond scent had told her everything she needed to know—even if it couldn't be proven yet.

"The cookie was in one of your bakery boxes, Faye." Luke's voice was gentle but firm. "With your logo. Your packaging."

"I didn't send her that cookie." Faye kept her voice steady. "I haven't made deliveries in days. I've been preparing for the Ball."

"I believe you." He held up a hand. "Personally, I believe you. But professionally..." He sighed, rubbing the back of his neck. "You have to understand the position I'm in... and the position you're in. The murder weapon—if that's what it is—came from your establishment. Or at least, it was made to look that way. And you identified it."

"Half the town has my boxes, Luke." She met his eyes. "Charlotte and Oliver were carrying three of them when they left Kent's shop yesterday. Rose picked up an order for the Historical Society. Even Kent bought cookies for his staff. Anyone could have used my packaging."

"Which is exactly why someone chose it," Luke said quietly. "Your boxes are everywhere. Trusted. Familiar. No one would think twice about seeing one at Beacon Hall."

"The front door," Luke said, glancing back toward the foyer. "Was it open when you arrived?"

"Ajar. A few inches." Faye frowned. "I thought Arthur had left it open for me, since I was expected. But he wasn't expecting me at all."

Luke turned to Arthur, who stood nearby looking shattered. "And you received a text from Henry about the door?"

"That's right." Arthur still looked shaken. "Henry said he'd come back from the framer's—I'd sent him to pick up new display cases for the Victorian Ball—and found the front door standing open. He texted me immediately. I left my meeting and came straight here."

"What time was that?"

"His text came at 3:52 P.M. I arrived perhaps ten minutes later."

Luke made a note. "So between whenever the door was opened and 3:52 P.M., someone came and went." He turned to Faye. "I'll need your phone. We can check the carrier records, see if that message actually originated from Arthur's device or if someone spoofed the number."

"Spoofed?"

"Made it look like it came from his number when it didn't. It's not as hard as people think." Luke's expression was thoughtful. "Actually, this could help us. If someone went to the trouble of faking a message to lure you here, they left a trail. Digital breadcrumbs."

"So this is good news?" Faye asked.

"It means whoever did this isn't as clever as they think they are." A hint of satisfaction crossed Luke's face. "They wanted to frame you, but they overplayed their hand. A simple frame job—just the bakery box—might have worked. But faking texts? That's traceable. That's a mistake."

Faye felt some of the tension ease from her shoulders. Not much, but some.

A mistake. The killer made a mistake.

It was a small comfort, but she'd take it.

Then came the words she'd been dreading.

"The café," Luke said. "I have to close it pending investigation. We need to examine your supplies, your packaging, your inventory. Make sure nothing else has been tampered with."

The words hit her like a physical blow. The café was her livelihood, her identity, her connection to this community she'd fought so hard to become part of. And now, during the busiest week of the year.

"For how long?"

"I don't know. Until we can clear you as a suspect, or until we find evidence pointing elsewhere."

"And Faye?" Luke's eyes held hers. "Margaret was killed because she knew something. And now you may know it too. Be careful. Stay close to people you trust."

———

SHE SHOULDN'T BE piecing things together. She knew that. Luke had told her to stay out of it, and she'd nodded and said all the right things.

But her eyes kept drifting to the clipboard hanging on a hook just inside the archive door.

The sign-in log. Anyone with archive access was required to log their visits when working unsupervised—early mornings, evenings, weekends. Faye had signed it herself a few times, back when she was researching Alice Whitford's recipe collection and Arthur had trusted her with a temporary key.

While Luke conferred with his officers near Margaret's body, Faye drifted toward the door. She wasn't touching anything. She was just... looking.

Her gaze snagged on something else first—a piece of paper beneath the reading table, partially hidden by the fallen lamp. It had landed face-down, but one corner was visible, and on it she could see the edge of familiar handwriting.

Margaret's handwriting.

Faye crouched lower, tilting her head to read without disturbing the scene. Three words, scrawled in Margaret's hasty script:

Archive key copied —

The sentence was cut off, the rest hidden.

Archive key copied. Who had Margaret been writing about?

She straightened and turned her attention to the sign-in log. Her eyes scanned the columns, looking for recent entries.

Arthur Whitford's neat signature appeared regularly. Henry Lawson, several times a week. Margaret herself, of course—her cramped handwriting filled multiple lines, sometimes with notes in the margins about which documents she'd accessed.

"Margaret was thorough," Faye thought. "She documented everything."

Including, perhaps, whatever had gotten her killed.

Rose Fairweather's name appeared three times in the past week alone—more frequently than usual. And this morning's entry showed she'd arrived at 8:15 A.M. and left at 9:47 A.M.

She was here this morning. She might have been one of the last people to see Margaret alive.

Faye's eyes moved down the list.

Kent Blake. She blinked. Kent wasn't on the Historical Society board—she remembered him mentioning once, with a tightness in his voice, that Arthur had declined his application years ago. Something about "conflicts of interest" with his exclusive right to cater weddings at the Beacon Hall. The rejection still seemed to sting.

Yet here was his signature, appearing several times over the past month.

A small notation in the margin caught her eye: "KB - Chemical preservation consultant. Facility upgrade."

Of course. Kent's expertise extended beyond wedding cakes. He knew his way around chemicals—the compounds that preserved delicate sugar work, the substances that protected fragile materials from decay. Beacon Hall was updating their archival storage systems. They'd need someone who understood how to protect aging documents from deterioration.

"Someone who understood chemistry."

Faye's mind flickered to the bitter almond scent still hanging in the air. She pushed the thought away. She was speculating. Kent was a respected businessman, a pillar of the community. Just because he knew about chemicals didn't mean…

Her eyes caught another familiar name, two weeks back: P. Grayson - Antiques Appraisal.

Three people. Three people beyond the regular staff who had signed into the archives recently. Three people who had been in her café this week, who had carried her distinctive bakery boxes out the door.

Rose, who was here this morning and had seemed more flustered than grieved when she saw Margaret.

Kent, with his chemistry expertise and his old grudge against Arthur.

And Peter, with his antiques connections.

She stopped herself.

You're not a detective, Faye. You're a baker who found a body.

But Margaret's unfinished note haunted her. Archive key copied —

Had Margaret discovered that someone had unauthorized access? Or had she discovered what one of these authorized visitors was really looking for?

"Faye?" Luke's voice made her jump. "We're ready to take your preliminary statement."

She stepped away from the clipboard, her mind still churning.

Three names. Three sets of questions.

And somewhere among them, a killer who had gone to a lot of trouble to make her look guilty.

"They made a mistake," she reminded herself. "And I'm going to figure out what it was."

<hr>

"WE'LL NEED MORE detailed statements from each of you tomorrow," Luke announced to the group gathered in the parlor. "For now, Beacon Hall is a crime scene. No one enters until my team has finished processing. Each of you please make an appointment with my officers to come to the station tomorrow.

Rose's hand flew to her chest. "But Ebenezer—the goose. He's in the back garden. I can't just leave him here."

Luke sighed. "Take the goose, Rose Fairweather. But nothing else leaves this building."

Faye gathered Tiny's leash, desperate to escape the oppressive weight of the crime scene. "Am I free to go?"

Luke met her eyes. Something unreadable passed between them. "For now. But Faye..." He paused," glancing at the other officers. "I'll need to speak with you later this evening. At your home, if that's acceptable."

It wasn't a request. Faye nodded and walked out into the cold December air, Tiny pressed close to her side.

———

THE PAINTED LADY, Faye's restored Victorian home, on Ocean Street glowed with warm light as Faye pulled into the driveway. She sat for a moment, hands still gripping the steering wheel, trying to compose herself before going inside. Tiny whined softly and pressed his nose against Faye's neck.

"I know, good boy. I know."

Dixie must have been watching from the window, because the front door flew open before Faye reached the porch steps. The teenager's face was pale with worry.

"Aunt Faye! Mom called and told me what happened. Are you okay? Is it true about Margaret Ellis?" Rose called mom because of the goose. Ebenezer is coming here.

Faye pulled Dixie into a hug, holding on perhaps a moment longer than necessary. "I'm okay, sweetheart. Shaken, but okay."

"Mom's on her way over. She's bringing soup." Dixie pulled back, her eyes searching Faye's face. "She said—she said Rose told her you found the body."

"I did." Faye guided them both inside. "Let's not talk about it right now, okay? I just need to sit down."

They settled in the kitchen, Faye's hands wrapped around a cup of tea she didn't remember making. Tiny lay on his sofa, his dark eyes blinking at her, offering quiet comfort.

The doorbell rang.

"I'll get it," Dixie said, jumping up. "That's probably Mom."

But the voice that echoed from the front hall wasn't Tessa's.

━━━

A COMMOTION at the front door made them look up—honking, footsteps, and a familiar voice.

"It's okay, buddy. Almost there. Just a few more steps."

Faye rose and walked to the entryway to join Dixie. Through the glass, they could see Evan Doyle coaxing a very indignant Ebenezer up the porch steps. The goose waddled reluctantly, honking his displeasure at every stair, while Evan murmured encouragements like a man negotiating with a toddler.

Faye stood by Dixie as she opened the door. "Evan? What on earth."

"Faye! Hey!" Evan's face was flushed from cold and effort. "Rose Fairweather flagged me down outside Beacon Hall. She needed help getting this guy somewhere safe, and she said you might take him?" He gestured at Ebenezer, who had planted himself on the welcome mat and was glaring at all of them with beady orange eyes. "He wouldn't get in her car. Wouldn't get in mine either, at first. But I bribed him with some bread from the Lobsta Shack I had that fell out of a deliver box. He eventually cooperated."

Ebenezer honked as if to dispute this characterization of events.

"Hey there, Ebenezer." Dixie crouched down to his level. "Remember me?"

The goose's feathers settled slightly. He honked again—softer this time—and took a tentative step toward her.

"He likes you," Evan said, sounding relieved.

Headlights swept across the front yard as a car pulled into

the driveway. Rose Fairweather emerged, her designer coat askew and her usually immaculate hair escaping its pins. She hurried up the walk, pulling off gloves that bore distinct beak-shaped tares.

"Thank God you're home." Rose stopped at the threshold, keeping a wary distance from Ebenezer. "I cannot deal with this creature. He bit my gloves. Twice. When I tried to put him in my car, he went for my hair." She touched her disheveled chignon with dismay.

"Come in," Faye said. "Both of you. It's freezing."

Rose hesitated—just for a moment—before stepping inside. Her eyes darted around the entryway, taking in the cozy warmth, the recently decorated Christmas tree, the normalcy of it all. She lingered. It was a sweet picture of a life that was foreign to her.

Rose turned and said "Beacon Hall is closed indefinitely. It's a crime scene, as you know, and I'm Ebenezer's designated caretaker, but I certainly can't keep him at my apartment. He'd terrorize my cat."

"Of course he can stay here," Faye said. "I've got a fenced backyard and a shelter that should work."

"Evan" Faye said, "you can take Ebenezer through the kitchen to the back porch."

"I'll open the porch door," Dixie ran ahead.

Rose stood in the entryway, fidgeting with her torn gloves, her eyes not quite meeting Faye's.

Faye, feeling exhausted and not very social, said "Is there something else, Rose?"

"I just—" Rose glanced toward the kitchen, then lowered her voice. "What did the police say? About how Margaret... about what happened?"

"They're still investigating."

"Yes, but did they say anything about—" Rose stopped, pressing her lips together. "About suspects? About who might have..."

Faye studied her. Rose Fairweather was normally the picture of composure—tailored clothes, perfect posture, every hair in place. Right now she looked like she'd been through a wind tunnel, and her questions had a sharp, anxious edge.

"Luke didn't share any theories with me," Faye said carefully. "Why do you ask?"

"No reason. I just—poor Margaret. I keep thinking about this morning, when I saw her. She was excited about something she'd found in the land records. Said she'd found the connection—the one that tied everything together." Rose's hands twisted together. "She mentioned a name... Rosewell? Does that mean anything to you?"

Faye kept her expression neutral, but her pulse quickened. Rosewell. The same name she'd seen in Margaret's notebook, connected to all those shell company transfers.

"I don't think so," she lied. "What else did Margaret say?"

"Nothing specific. She was always careful that way—wouldn't speculate until she'd verified everything. I didn't think to ask more. I was in a hurry, had errands to run, and I left her there alone, and now..." Rose's voice cracked. She pressed a hand to her mouth.

"It's not your fault," Faye said automatically.

But her mind was racing. Rose had been there this morning. Rose had heard Margaret mention Rosewell by name. Rose had left her "alone"—and now Rose was very, very interested in what the police knew.

Was this grief? Or something else?

Evan shifted awkwardly by the front door. "I should probably head out. Uncle Yves is expecting me." He paused. "Faye—I'm really sorry about what happened. Margaret Ellis was always nice to me when I made deliveries to Beacon Hall. She'd ask about my classes and stuff." His young face was troubled. "I hope they catch whoever did it."

"Thank you, Evan. And thank you for helping with Ebenezer." Faye was joined by Rose.

After Evan's truck disappeared down the street, Rose seemed to collect herself. She straightened her coat, put her hair behind her ear, and manufactured a smile.

"I really must go. This has all been so—" She paused, and for a moment something flickered across her face. Then the mask settled back into place. "So terrible. I still can't believe it."

"Rose," Faye said quietly. "If you know something—anything—about what Margaret found, you should tell Luke. Not me. Luke."

Rose went very still.

"I don't know what you mean," she said. But her voice was too light, too careful. "I'm just upset. We all are."

She was out the door before Faye could respond, walking quickly to her car without looking back.

Faye stood in the doorway, watching the taillights disappear down Ocean Street.

What are you afraid of, Rose? What do you know?

———

AFTER ROSE LEFT, Faye and Dixie found Ebenezer back inside. He waddled with surprising dignity, honking softly at points of interest—the kitchen radiator, Tiny's water bowl—as if conducting an inspection.

They ushered him back outside. The back yard was small but secure, the wooden fence tall enough to discourage escape. The shelter in the corner—once a potting shed, now mostly empty—had a solid roof and walls that would block the wind. Faye had lined it with old blankets last winter when a stray cat had taken up temporary residence.

Ebenezer surveyed his new domain with a critical eye. He pecked at the frozen grass, investigated the shelter's interior, and finally settled near the back door with a satisfied honk.

Tiny had followed them outside and now stood watching

the goose with patient curiosity. After a moment, the two seemed to reach an understanding—a mutual acknowledgment of territory and respect.

"He's going to be fine here," Dixie said, grinning despite the weight of the day. "Look at him. He's already acting like he owns the place."

Despite everything, Faye felt the corners of her mouth twitch. "That's geese for you. Give them an inch..."

"They take the whole backyard." Dixie laughed softly. "I'll make sure he has water. And maybe some of that bread Evan mentioned?"

"There's some bread in the pantry. Stale stuff I was going to throw out."

As Dixie headed inside, Faye stood in the cold December evening, watching Ebenezer settle into his new home. Tiny pressed against her leg, warm and solid.

An unlikely menagerie, she thought. A Dane and a goose.

But somehow, standing there in the fading light, it felt right. Like one small thing, at least, had been set in order amid all the chaos.

⊏⊐

THE DOORBELL RANG AGAIN, and this time it was Tessa, carrying a pot of soup and wearing an expression of fierce concern. She set the pot on the stove, wrapped Faye in a tight hug, and then stepped back to assess her.

"You look terrible."

"Thanks."

"I mean it. Sit down. Eat something." Tessa began ladling soup into bowls. "Dixie, set the table. We're all going to have dinner and pretend the world isn't falling apart."

They gathered around the kitchen table—Faye, Tessa, and Dixie—while Tiny claimed the kitchen sofa as his own, and

Ebenezer explored the corners of the backyard with investigative honks.

For a few minutes, the warmth of the soup and the comfort of family pushed the horrors of the afternoon to the edges of Faye's mind.

Tessa reached across the table and squeezed her hand. "It's going to be okay. Luke will find whoever did this."

Faye nodded, but the words felt hollow. The image of Margaret's body wouldn't leave her—the scattered papers, the bakery box with her logo, the bitter scent of almonds.

A knock at the door made them all jump.

———

FAYE ROSE SLOWLY, already knowing who it would be. She opened the door to find Luke standing on her porch, his face grave in the yellow glow of the porch light. Snow dusted his shoulders.

"May I come in?"

She stepped aside. Luke entered, nodding politely to Tessa and Dixie, but his attention remained fixed on Faye. From the backyard, Ebenezer honked a greeting.

"Is that—" Luke blinked. "Is that the goose from Beacon Hall?"

"Rose dropped him off," Faye said. "What is it, Luke? What's wrong?"

He removed his hat, turning it in his hands—a nervous gesture she'd never seen from him before. "I need to speak with you about the investigation. Officially."

Tessa stood. "Dixie, let's give them some privacy. Help me clean up."

"But Mom—"

"Now, Dixie."

The two retreated to the kitchen, though Faye suspected

Tessa's ears were straining to hear every word. She gestured Luke toward the living room, and they sat across from each other—she in her grandmother's wingback chair, he on the edge of the settee.

"I've assigned Officer Burke to stand watch outside your café," Luke said. "No one goes in or out until my team has finished."

Faye stared at her hands, clasped tight in her lap. *The Heirloom Table Café*, shuttered. Her name connected to a murder. Everything she'd built in Butternut Cove, suddenly fragile as spun glass.

"I'll see you at the station tomorrow. Nine o'clock."

She walked him to the door. On the threshold, he paused and turned back.

"For what it's worth," he said, his voice low enough that only she could hear, "I don't think you did this. Not for a second."

Then he was gone, disappearing into the falling snow.

———

LATER THAT NIGHT, after Tessa had gone home and Dixie had reluctantly gone to bed, Faye sat in her kitchen. The house was quiet except for the tick of the grandmother clock and the soft sounds of her unlikely menagerie settling in for the night.

Tiny had settled onto his kitchen sofa nearby, his great head draped over the arm, quietly keeping her company. Through the window, she could see Ebenezer in the backyard shelter, his head tucked under one wing.

"What did you find, Margaret?" Faye whispered to the empty room. "What was worth dying for?"

She thought of the scattered papers—property deeds, survey maps, transfer documents. Land records going back generations. Margaret had spent her life preserving Butternut

Cove's history. Had she stumbled onto something that someone wanted buried?

"*Archive key copied —*"

The unfinished note haunted her. Who had Margaret been writing about? And why had someone gone to such trouble to make Faye look guilty—not just her bakery box, but the fake text, luring her to the scene?

"They made a mistake," Luke had said. "Digital breadcrumbs."

The Victorian Ball was in two days. The whole town would gather at Beacon Hall—if it was even still happening—dancing and celebrating while a killer walked among them.

Five names circled in her mind. Rose, with her nervous questions and her too-quick departure. Kent, with his chemistry knowledge and his old grudge. Peter, with his antiques appraisals and his access to her bakery boxes. Arthur and Henry had full access to the archives and looked shocked and overly concerned was this grief or were they concealing something.

Had one of them killed Margaret. Had one of them framed her.

Her café was closed. Her reputation was at stake. And someone had murdered her friend, using her name to do it.

Faye stroked Tiny's fur and made a silent promise.

"I will find out the truth. For Margaret. For myself. For this town."

She would be careful. She would be discreet. But she would not sit by while someone destroyed everything she loved.

Tomorrow, she would go to the police station like a cooperative citizen. She would answer their questions and give her fingerprints and play the part they expected.

But she would also start asking questions of her own.

Outside, snow continued to fall, blanketing Butternut Cove in white. It looked peaceful. Pure.

But Faye knew better now. Beneath the postcard prettiness, someone had secrets worth killing for.

Tiny shifted, pressing closer, and Faye let her hand rest on the dog's warm fur. From the backyard, Ebenezer honked softly in his sleep.

It was the first time she whispered the truth instead of shouting I'm fine.

6

Fingerprints and Whispers

FRIDAY, DECEMBER 19TH.

The Butternut Cove Police Station smelled of burned coffee and accumulated dust. Faye sat in a plastic chair outside Luke's office. Tiny rested his head on her knee, the Dane's warmth a small comfort against the institutional chill. Officers moved through the open office space with studied purpose. None of them met her eyes. She'd arrived early. Old habit. Her mother had drilled punctuality into her like a religious conviction, and even now—sitting in a police station while her café remained sealed behind yellow tape—Faye couldn't bring herself to be late.

Tiny shifted, lifting his massive head from Faye's knee and glanced at her face. Those dark, knowing eyes seemed to say: *I'm here. Whatever happens, I'm here.*

The door to Luke's office opened, and he appeared, looking like he hadn't slept. His tie was slightly crooked, and there were shadows beneath his eyes that hadn't been there two days ago.

"Faye." He gestured her inside, his gaze dropping briefly to Tiny. "He can come too."

His office was small and tidy, the walls lined with commendations and a single photograph of Whale's Tail lighthouse at sunset. Someone had strung a modest garland of pine along the window frame, and a ceramic Christmas tree—the kind with little colored bulbs that lit up—sat on the filing cabinet. Even here, the season insisted on making itself known.

"The fingerprinting is a formality," Luke said, settling behind his desk. "Standard procedure for anyone connected to an active investigation."

"Connected to." Faye kept her voice even. "That's a diplomatic way to say 'suspect.'"

Luke's sighed. "You're not—" He stopped, ran a hand through his hair. "Officially, everyone who was at Beacon Hall yesterday is a person of interest. You, Arthur, Henry, Rose. We're processing everyone."

"But my bakery box was next to the body."

"Yes." He met her eyes, and she saw the conflict there—the warring with whatever else he felt. "It was."

Tiny pressed closer against Faye's leg, a low rumble in his chest—not quite a growl, more a sound of solidarity.

The fingerprinting took less than ten minutes. A bored technician rolled Faye's fingers across an ink pad, pressed them to cards, handed her a wet wipe that smelled of chemicals and didn't quite remove the black stains from her fingertips. Faye found herself staring at her hands as she walked back to Luke's office. *Marked.* That's what she was now. Marked.

"I need to take your formal statement," Luke said when she returned. He had a notepad ready, a recorder on the desk between them. "Walk me through yesterday again. From the beginning."

So she did. The morning at the café. Arthur and Henry's visit. The walk to Kent's shop with Tessa and Tiny. Rose and Charlotte and the blue Bentley. Callie's delivery. Margaret's terrified visit—the hidden note, the fear in her eyes.

"The note," Luke said, leaning forward. "You said Margaret hid a note in your cookbook. At the café."

"Yes. Mrs. Beeton's—my grandmother's copy. She said she slipped something inside the day before. In case..." Faye's voice caught. "In case something happened to her."

Luke was already reaching for his phone. "I'll get authorization to retrieve it. That note could be crucial evidence."

He made the call while Faye waited, Tiny leaning into her like an anchor. She watched Luke's expression shift—from hopeful to frustrated to resigned—as the conversation progressed.

"Chief says he'll work on it," Luke said, setting down the phone. "The café is still an active crime scene and we are short staffed. And even then, it has to go through proper channels."

"How long must we wait?" "Margaret left that note because she knew she was in danger. Whatever's in it—"

"I know." Luke's frustration was palpable. "But I can't cut corners. Not on this. Not when..." He didn't finish the sentence, but she understood. Not when you're already a suspect.

"What about my café?" The question came out smaller than she intended. "When can I reopen?"

Luke's expression softened. "I'm pushing for Monday. Maybe Sunday if we're lucky. We've finished processing most of the evidence—your baked goods, packaging materials, anything that might have been contaminated. The health department needs to clear the kitchen."

"The Ball is tomorrow night." Faye heard the edge in her own voice. "I was supposed to compete in the dessert contest. My puddings are locked in there, along with all my supplies, my equipment —"

"I know." Luke sighed. "I'm sorry, Faye. I wish I could do more."

She stood, gathering Tiny's leash. There was nothing more to say. Her livelihood was behind yellow tape, her reputation in tatters, and somewhere in Butternut Cove, a killer was walking free.

"Faye." Luke's voice stopped her at the door. "Be careful. Margaret knew something that got her killed. And you were the last person we are aware of that she talked to."

The words hung in the air between them, heavy with implication.

"I'll be in touch," he added, more gently. "About the note. About everything."

She nodded and walked out into the December morning, Tiny padding silently at her side.

⊏⊐

THE COLD HIT her like a reproach. She nodded and went outside into the December morning, with Tiny silently beside her.

Faye walked through town with Tiny, past the harbor where fishing boats bobbed in the grey water, their masts strung with Christmas lights that swayed in the salt breeze. The air was damp and sharp, carrying the scent of pine and brine. A light snow drifted lazily from the pewter sky—more suggestion than storm, the way it always was this close to the ocean.

The streets were busy with Christmas shoppers, the storefronts glittering with lights and garlands. Celia Shand's balsam wreaths hung on every door, festive and fragrant. *O Come All Ye Faithful* drifted from the bookshop's open door. Butternut Cove at its most picturesque.

Except.

Conversations died when she approached. Mabel Thornton—who bought scones from the café every Tuesday without fail—crossed the street rather than walk past her. Two women from the Historical Society, whom Faye knew, were whispering and watching her closely.

She caught fragments as she passed:

...her bakery box, right there beside the body...

...only been here a few years, you know, not really one of us...

...always thought there was something off about her...

Faye kept walking, her chin up, her grip tight on Tiny's leash. She would not give them the satisfaction of seeing her crumble.

Tiny, for his part, walked with extra dignity, as if determined to demonstrate that his human was worthy of respect even if these small-minded townspeople couldn't see it.

As they passed *The Heirloom Table Café* Faye couldn't help but slow, couldn't help but look.

Yellow crime scene tape stretched across the front door, bright and garish against the café's cheerful green trim. The Christmas wreath she'd hung just last week—pine boughs and dried oranges and cinnamon sticks—still hung there, incongruously festive above the police seal. Through the window, she could see the darkened interior, the empty display cases, the espresso machine gleaming dully in the thin winter light.

Her sanctuary. Her second chance. The place where she'd rebuilt herself after losing everything.

Now a crime scene.

Tiny whined softly and pressed against her leg.

"I know, honey," Faye murmured. "I know."

———

HOME WAS QUIET. Too quiet.

Dixie was at school—Tessa had insisted on keeping things as normal as possible—and the only sounds were the tick of the grandmother clock and the occasional indignant honk from Ebenezer, who had claimed the enclosed back porch as his additional territory. The goose had settled in with remarkable speed, as if he always belonged here.

Faye made coffee she didn't drink. Straightened pillows that didn't need straightening. Stood at the window and watched the street, where neighbors walked past with their dogs and their shopping bags, casting glances at her house that they probably thought were subtle.

She kept thinking and reviewing again and again. She had noticed Peter Grayson's antique shop across the square. Something looked different about it today. She squinted—were those SALE signs in the windows? In all her years in Butternut Cove, she'd never seen Peter discount anything. He was notorious for his prices, insisting that quality commanded premium value.

Strange. But then, everything felt strange this week.

Tiny settled on his sofa by the radiator, watching Faye with concerned eyes. Even the dog knew something was wrong.

The Ball was tomorrow night. The Dessert competition she'd been preparing for all month. Her chance to prove herself to the Historical Society, to solidify her place in Butternut Cove, to show that she belonged here.

And now?

Her puddings were locked behind crime scene tape. Her kitchen was sealed. She had no supplies, no equipment, no way to compete even if she wanted to.

And part of her wondered if she even should. Part of her wondered if showing up at the Ball—at an event celebrating

Butternut Cove's history while the town whispered that she might be a murderer—was the height of audacity.

The doorbell rang.

Tiny's head came up. He didn't bark—service dogs rarely did—but his tail gave a single, cautious wag.

Faye opened the door to find Callie Sweet on her doorstep, Jaxson at her side and Fig in her shoulder carrier. Callie was carrying a basket covered with a red-checked cloth, and her face held the determined expression of someone who had come to do battle.

"Don't argue," Callie said, pushing past her into the house. "I've brought soup, bread, and a plan. In that order."

———

THE SOUP WAS chicken and dumplings, rich and warming. The bread was Callie's signature sourdough, still slightly warm from the oven. Faye ate more than she'd expected to, suddenly aware that she hadn't had anything since yesterday's rushed dinner.

Tiny had claimed his sofa near the hearth, already drifting toward sleep, while Jaxson sprawled on the floor by the radiator, soaking up every bit of heat it offered. Fig had stationed herself on the back of the sofa, surveying the room with the air of a queen holding court. From the back porch, Ebenezer offered an occasional honk of commentary.

"Now," Callie said, setting down her own empty bowl. "The plan."

"Callie, I appreciate this, but…"

"No buts." Callie held up a hand. "I've been where you are. Maybe not exactly—nobody accused me of murder—but I know what it's like to be the outsider. The one people whisper about. The one who doesn't quite belong." Her eyes softened. "This town took a while to accept me, too. But it did. And it will accept you again, once this mess is sorted out."

"The mess," Faye said bitterly, "is that someone used my bakery boxes to deliver poison. My name is on the packaging. My cookies were found next to Margaret's body."

"Which means someone is trying to frame you. Which means someone else is the killer." Callie leaned forward. "And the best way to prove that is to show up. Hold your head high. Compete in that pudding contest like you planned. Don't let them see you hide."

"I can't compete. My café is sealed. My puddings, my supplies, everything…"

"Which is why," Callie said, a smile spreading across her face, "you're going to use my kitchen."

Faye stared at her. "What?"

"*How Sweet It Is.* My kitchen. It's got everything you need —ovens, mixers, all the basics. I've already got most of the ingredients you'll need for figgy pudding, and what I don't have, we can pick up from the general store." Callie's eyes were bright with determination. "We'll bake tonight. Together. You'll have a pudding ready for tomorrow's competition if I have to stay up until midnight helping you."

"Callie…" Faye's voice caught. "Why are you doing this?"

"Because that's what we do in Butternut Cove." Callie reached across the table and squeezed her hand. "The real Butternut Cove, I mean. Not the gossips and the whispers. The people who actually matter—we take care of each other."

For the first time since finding Margaret's body, Faye felt tears prick her eyes. Not from grief this time, but from gratitude.

"I don't know what to say."

"Say yes." Callie stood, already gathering their bowls. "And then get your coat. We've got pudding to make."

HOW SWEET *It Is was warm and fragrant, filled with the scent of yeast and something spicy—gingerbread, maybe, or the mulled cider Callie kept simmering on the back burner. Christmas garlands wound around the display cases, and a small tree in the corner twinkled with white lights, casting a muted glow over the closed bakery.*

Tiny occupied his usual sofa near the wall, long legs folded beneath him as he calmly observed the room. On the floor beside him, Jaxson curled up contentedly, while Fig claimed the top of the flour bin as her throne.

"Allison," Callie called toward the back. "Come meet Faye properly."

A young woman emerged from the storeroom, wiping her hands on her apron. She was in her mid-twenties, with honey-brown hair pulled back in a practical ponytail and the slightly anxious expression of someone still trying to find her footing. Her eyes widened when she saw Faye.

"Oh! You're—I mean, I've heard—" She flushed. "Sorry. That came out wrong. I'm Allison. Allison Day."

"It's all right." Faye managed a smile. "I imagine everyone's heard something by now."

"I don't believe any of it," Allison said quickly. "For what it's worth. I haven't been here long, but I can tell—you're not..." She trailed off, apparently realizing that finishing the sentence with "a murderer" might not be the most tactful choice.

"Thank you," Faye said, and meant it.

"Allison's been a lifesaver," Callie said, pulling out mixing bowls and measuring cups. "Even if she's still figuring out the difference between baking powder and baking soda." She shot her assistant a fond look. "She's better with deliveries and bookkeeping. And she'll be helping serve at the Ball tomorrow."

"I'm more of a horse person, honestly," Allison admitted. "But Butternut Cove doesn't have many stables. When someone at a regatta mentioned this town—said it was quiet, peaceful, a good place to start over—I figured I'd try something new."

"Starting over." Faye understood that better than Allison knew. "It's hard, isn't it? Coming somewhere new. Trying to belong."

Allison nodded, something easing in her expression. "It is. But this place—once people get to know you—it's worth it. At least, that's what Callie keeps telling me."

"She's right." Faye pulled her grandmother's recipe from her bag—she'd memorized it years ago, but having the faded index card felt like a talisman. "Now. Let's make some figgy pudding."

***

CALLIE SURVEYED the ingredients Faye had spread across her bakery counter with undisguised skepticism.

"Faye, I don't want to be discouraging, but a proper figgy pudding takes weeks. The fruit needs to macerate—"

"I know." Faye reached into her canvas bag and produced a quart mason jar, the glass dark with brandy-soaked fruit. "That's why I brought this."

Callie took the jar, holding it up to the light. Inside, figs, raisins, currants, and candied peel glistened in amber liquid, the fruit swollen and glossy from months of patient soaking.

Allison leaned in for a closer look. "My friend Claire in London makes a Christmas pudding every year. I visited her last December and watched the whole process." She studied the jar with newfound interest. "Claire's fruit had been soaking since October, but yours looks even darker. How long has this been steeping?"

"The Christmas before last." Faye smiled at their expressions. "My grandmother always kept extra macerated fruit in the cellar. 'Insurance,' she called it. After Derek and Jenny..." She paused, the familiar ache pressing against her ribs. "I couldn't face making a pudding that year. Or the next. But I couldn't bring myself to throw the fruit away either. Gran's voice in my head, I suppose."

"Two years of steeping." called unscrewed the lid and inhaled, her eyes widening. "Faye, this smells incredible. The brandy's had all that time to really penetrate the fruit."

"Claire's pudding was amazing, and hers only soaked for two months." Allison's eyes were bright with understanding. "If two months makes that much difference, two years must be…"

"That's the secret Gran never told anyone." Faye began measuring flour into a bowl. "A proper pudding isn't just about the steaming—it's about the fruit having time to absorb the spirits until every bite carries that warmth. Most competition puddings are made on Stir-Up Sunday, maybe six weeks of maceration. This fruit has had over two years."

"But you still have to steam it," Allison said. "Claire's took forever—she started at dawn and it wasn't done until late afternoon. We don't have that kind of time."

"Hours we have." Faye glanced at the clock—just past seven. "Traditional steaming is six to eight hours, but Gran had a shortcut for emergencies." She pulled a small notebook from her bag, the pages soft with age and spotted with ancient butter stains. "We steam it for four hours tonight to set the structure, then give it a boost."

"A boost?" Callie studied the handwritten recipe.

"Fifteen minutes in a low microwave to warm it through without drying it out, then another hour of steaming tomorrow morning to develop that deep mahogany color and let the flavors meld." Faye tapped the notebook. "Gran called it 'waking up the pudding.' The microwave heats it evenly from the inside, and then the final steam caramelizes the outside and marries everything together."

"Claire reheated hers in the microwave on Christmas Day," Allison said slowly, working through the logic. "Covered with a damp cloth. She said all the old-timers do it that way now—it's faster than re-steaming for two hours."

"Same principle." Faye began creaming butter and dark brown sugar with practiced efficiency. "The microwave gets the heat moving through the dense center; the steam finishes the job on the outside. It won't have quite the density of a pudding that's been aged for months after steaming, but with fruit this well-steeped?" She smiled. "It'll taste like Christmas morning."

"And if Kent Blake asks how you managed it overnight?" called asked.

Faye's smile turned mischievous. "Then I'll tell him the truth: the fruit's been preparing for this moment for two years. It just didn't know it yet." She began folding the jewel-dark fruit into the batter, the scent of brandy and Christmas spices rising like a promise. "Neither did I."

They worked through the afternoon and into the evening, the kitchen filling with the rich scent of dried figs and brandy and warm spices.

Callie handled the technical aspects—her ovens ran differently than Faye's, and she knew their quirks. Allison fetched ingredients and washed bowls and asked questions that revealed how little she knew about baking and how eager she was to learn.

And Faye—Faye lost herself in the work. In the familiar rhythm of measuring and mixing, of folding and stirring, of watching the batter come together into something rich and dark and fragrant. This was what she knew. This was who she was. Not a suspect. Not an outsider. Just a woman who loved to bake, carrying on a tradition that stretched back through her grandmother and her grandmother's mother before her.

"*My grandmother used to say that figgy pudding was love made visible,*" Faye said, pouring the batter into the prepared mold. "All those hours of preparation, all that care—you can taste it in every bite."

"That's beautiful," Allison said softly.

"It's also a lot of work." Callie laughed, wiping flour from her cheek. "But worth it. Always worth it."

The pudding went into the steamer, and the three of them sat around Callie's small kitchen table, drinking tea and eating the gingerbread cookies Callie had made that morning. Outside, the December darkness had fallen early, and Christmas lights twinkled through the window from the shops across the street.

Steam rose from the pot in lazy curls, carrying the scent of brandy and figs through the kitchen. Faye watched it for a moment, thinking of all the Christmas puddings she'd helped her grandmother make—the ritual of it, the stirring and wishing, the way the whole house would smell of spices for days.

"You okay?" Callie asked softly.

"Yeah." Faye felt surprised to feel it. "I kept that jar because I couldn't let go. But maybe..." She watched the steam rise, carrying memories and brandy and something that felt almost like hope. "Maybe I was keeping it for exactly this moment. For when I was ready to make something sweet again."

Allison reached over and squeezed her hand. No words needed.

"I should tell you," Callie said carefully, "there's been talk about whether the Ball should still happen. After Margaret."

Faye looked up. "And?"

"Arthur insisted. He called an emergency meeting of the Historical Society Board this morning. They have petitioned the police chief and the chief inspector, he said Margaret would have wanted the traditions to continue. That canceling would be letting fear win." Callie paused. Arthur said the archives are still sealed—that's where... where it happened. But the rest of Beacon Hall is open. He asked that the Ball go on as planned."

Faye thought of Arthur, his warm handshake, his hints

about secrets in the archives. She thought of Margaret, terrified and disheveled, pressing that notebook into her hands. She thought of the note hidden in her cookbook, still locked behind crime scene tape, waiting to be read.

"Luke said they're bringing in extra officers," Callie continued. "Just in case. The whole town will be there. Safety in numbers, I suppose."

Safety in numbers. Or a killer hiding in plain sight.

Faye pushed the thought away. Tomorrow, she would go to the Ball. She would enter her figgy pudding in the dessert contest. She would hold her head high and let the whispers slide off her back.

And if someone tried to stop her—well. She'd spent years learning how to survive the worst life could throw at her. She wasn't about to let a murderer steal her grandmother's Christmas traditions.

━━

IT WAS NEARLY ten when Faye finally left *How Sweet It Is*, the figgy pudding safely cooling in Callie's kitchen, ready to be transported to Beacon Hall tomorrow. Tiny walked beside her through the quiet streets, past the darkened shops and the glowing Christmas lights, past the occasional couple hurrying home from dinner, past *The Heirloom Table Café* with its yellow tape gleaming faintly in the streetlight.

Home was warm and welcoming, Ebenezer settling down with a final sleepy honk as Faye checked his enclosure. Dixie had left a note on the kitchen counter: *Tessa picked me up for dinner. Home by 11. Don't worry. Love you.*

Faye stood at the window, looking out at the quiet street. Somewhere out there, a killer was sleeping peacefully or not. Somewhere out there, Margaret's murderer was making plans for tomorrow.

But so was she.

Tomorrow, the Victorian Ball. Tomorrow, the dessert competition. Tomorrow, she would walk into Beacon Hall with her head held high and her eyes wide open.

And maybe—just maybe—she would find the answers Margaret had died trying to uncover.

7

Friday Night Visitors
FRIDAY, DECEMBER 19TH.

Faye taking refuge in establishing order went to her kitchen and started to tidy up. The house was quiet. Dixie called and said she was staying with Tessa tonight. Apparently, she was exhausted from the weight of worry she was trying so hard not to show. Faye felt regretted the Dixie had been swept into all of this.

Ebenezer had settled in a crate on the back porch, his soft honks fading into sleep. Faithful Tiny remained awake, stretched out on his sofa by the radiator, watching Faye with those dark, knowing eyes.

Faye sat at the kitchen table, a cup of tea cooling beside her. She reached into her bag for a biscuit for Tiny and brushed against the edge of her notebook instead. She drew it out and stared at it, her thoughts slowing.

Margaret's notebook. How did it get there? Then she remembered. She had shoved it into in her bag yesterday—was it really only yesterday—when Margaret had pressed it into her hands and made her swear to keep it secret.

In the chaos of finding the body, the police station, the fingerprinting, the whispers, she'd forgotten about it. It was so small and her tote bag was so big. Would that explain the omission to Detective Grayson? It had sat unremembered in her bag through the execution of Callie's rescue plan, through the baking, through everything.

Now, with the figgy pudding safely cooling at How Sweet It Is and the Ball looming tomorrow, Faye finally had a moment to think. And what she was thinking was making her deeply uncomfortable.

She hadn't told Luke about the notebook; she hadn't remembered it.

In her formal statement, she'd mentioned Margaret's visit, her fear, the note hidden in the cookbook. But the notebook—the actual physical evidence Margaret had given her—she'd said nothing about. At first it was shock, genuine forgetfulness in the horror of finding Margaret's body. But now?

Now she was sitting here, holding it, knowing she should call Luke immediately.

But… not calling.

Tiny lifted his head, as if sensing Faye's unease. His tail thumped once against the floor—not judgment, just acknowledgment.

"I should turn it in," Faye said aloud. "It's evidence."

Tiny's expression seemed to say: *And yet?*

"And yet." Faye sighed. "If I give it to Luke, it becomes official evidence. It goes into a box somewhere. It gets processed and analyzed and filed away, and I never see it again. And maybe that's fine. Maybe that's right. But Margaret gave it to *me*. She trusted *me* with it. She said—"

She stopped, remembering Margaret's exact words: Keep this safe. Don't tell anyone you have it.

Don't tell anyone.

Faye opened the notebook.

———

FAYE OPENED the book at random. Now that she had an opportunity to look at it, it wasn't Margaret's notebook after all. It was Bee's. It had belonged to her grandmother.

Margaret's handwriting was small and precise, the script of a woman who'd spent decades cataloging historical documents. This section of the notebook was organized by date, going back five years. Each entry contained property descriptions, transfer dates, buyer names—most of which Faye didn't recognize. Shell companies, she assumed. The kind of anonymous entities that existed only on paper.

But as she turned the pages, patterns began to emerge.

The same dates appeared again and again—transfers clustered around town council meetings, zoning hearings, approval deadlines. The lighthouse restoration approval that Margaret had mentioned was there, circled in red, with a note in the margin: *Expedited. Who authorized?*

Faye turned more pages. Initials appeared throughout: P.G., C.S., H.L., others she couldn't decipher. Some circled, some crossed out, some with question marks. Margaret had been tracking something, piecing together a puzzle whose full picture Faye couldn't see.

And then, near the back of the notebook, she found a page startled her.

A list of properties. Harbor lots, waterfront parcels, commercial buildings along Ocean Street. Next to each one, a date and a name. Most of the names meant nothing to her—corporate entities, legal-sounding phrases.

But one name she recognized immediately.

Harper.

Faye stared at the entry. *Harper Family Trust—Lot 47, transferred 1987—see original deed.*

Lot 47. She had no idea what Lot 47 was or where it was located. But the Harper Family Trust—that was her family. Her father's family. The family that had deep roots in Butternut Cove, roots she'd only begun to understand since moving back here five years ago.

Arthur's words echoed in her memory: *I've discovered something in the archives that concerns both our families. Something that's been buried for a very long time.*

Was this what he'd meant? Something about her family's property? Something about Lot 47? She paused. Wasn't the number on the paper she picked up on the Cliffs?

She got up and crossed over to where she had left her coat on the arm of the sofa. There it was in her pocket, crumpled but clear... Lot 47.

Faye returned to the notebook and flipped through more pages, searching for context, but the notebook offered only fragments. Names and dates and cryptic notations. A puzzle with too many missing pieces.

As she closed the notebook, she paused to look at the front page and sat very still. It said this book belongs to Belinda Harper. She sat very still.

The notebook had belonged to Bee, to her grandmother, whose house Faye had inherited. Margaret had been killed for what she understood about all these facts. And now Faye was holding that same knowledge—but to her—incomplete, confusing, and dangerous. The notebook connected her family to whatever scheme Margaret had uncovered. If she turned it over to Luke, she'd be handing him evidence that might implicate her own relatives if not herself.

But if she didn't...

An idea began to form. A terrible, tempting idea.

Margaret must have found it in the archives, among Bee's donated papers.

If I hid it here, in this house, and it was "discovered" later... who would know the difference? It could be presented as something Bee had left behind. Something Faye found while cleaning out a closet.

No one had seen Margaret hand it to her. No one knew she had it.

Except...

Except her own conscience. And Tiny, whose dark eyes seemed to be asking: *Is that really who you are?*

The doorbell rang.

⸺

FAYE'S HEART LURCHED. Who would come by at—she checked the clock—nearly eleven on a Friday night?

She slipped the notebook into the kitchen drawer beneath a stack of dish towels and went to the door, Tiny walking beside her. Through the frosted glass, she could see two figures on the porch, their outlines distorted by the pattern but somehow familiar.

She opened the door.

"Surprise!"

Dean Flute stood on her doorstep, arms spread wide, grinning the same boyish grin he'd had since they were twelve years old. Beside him, his wife Anne was already moving forward for a hug, her red coat bright against the December darkness.

"Dean?" Faye blinked, certain she was hallucinating. "Anne? What are you—how are you—"

"Flew in this afternoon!" Dean swept her into a bear hug that lifted her off her feet. "We're performing at the Ball tomorrow—didn't Arthur tell you? He booked us months ago. Thought we'd surprise you tonight instead of waiting."

Anne was already inside, petting Tiny, who had abandoned all pretense of service-dog dignity and was wagging his tail with abandon. "We tried calling, but your phone went straight to voicemail. So, we just showed up. Hope that's okay?"

"Okay?" Faye felt tears prick her eyes. "It's wonderful. It's—come in, come in. I'll make tea. Or do you want something stronger? I think I have wine somewhere—"

She was babbling, she knew. But seeing Dean—Dean, her oldest friend, the boy she'd grown up with in Butternut Cove before her family moved away, the man who'd made it big in Nashville but never forgot where he came from—felt like a lifeline thrown to a drowning woman.

They settled into the living room, Tiny stretched out on the rug between them, Anne exclaiming over the Christmas decorations while Dean was already rummaging through the kitchen for snacks. It was so normal, so wonderfully normal, that Faye almost forgot the notebook hidden in the drawer, the murder, the whispers, all of it.

Almost.

"So," Dean said, returning with a plate of cookies—store-bought, not hers—and settling into the armchair by the fire. "Catch us up. What's new in Butternut Cove? The café still going strong?"

Faye's smile faltered. "You haven't heard."

Dean and Anne exchanged glances. "Heard what?" Anne asked carefully.

And so Faye told them. Everything. Margaret's fear. The body in the archives. Her bakery boxes at the crime scene with the bitter almond scent. The whispers, the fingerprinting, the café sealed behind yellow tape. She left out the notebook—that secret still felt too raw, too complicated—but everything else came pouring out.

When she finished, Dean was leaning forward, his performer's ease replaced by the sharp focus she remembered from their childhood. He'd always been like this—charming on the surface, surprisingly perceptive underneath.

"Someone's framing you," he said. It wasn't a question.

"That's what Callie said."

"Callie's right." Dean drummed his fingers on the arm of the chair, thinking. "Your packaging, your cookies—that's deliberate. Someone wanted the trail to lead to you. The question is why."

"Because Margaret came to see me," Faye said. "Because she trusted me with what she knew. Maybe the killer saw that. Maybe they think I know more than I do."

"Or," Anne said slowly, "maybe it's not about you at all. Maybe you're just... convenient. A newcomer. Someone the town would believe could be guilty."

The words stung because they were true. Three years in Butternut Cove, and she was still "the woman who moved into Bee Harper's place." Still an outsider. Still, someone the gossips could turn on when things went wrong.

"You said Margaret found something about property transfers," Dean said. "Land deals, zoning, that kind of thing?"

Faye nodded.

"I've seen this before." Dean's expression darkened. "Nashville, believe it or not. And a couple other towns where I've played. Developers come in, buy up property through shell companies, get friendly with local officials. By the time anyone realizes what's happening, they own half the town." He met her eyes. "Follow the money, Faye. Whoever killed Margaret—they're protecting something worth a lot more than a few harbor lots."

Follow the money.

Faye thought of the notebook in the kitchen drawer. The

shell companies. The initials. Lot 47 and the Harper Family Trust.

"There's something else," she said slowly. "Something I haven't told anyone."

Dean and Anne waited.

"My family is connected to this somehow. The Harpers. There's a property—Lot 47—that was transferred decades ago. I don't know what it means, but..." She trailed off. "Arthur said he wanted to talk to me about something. About my family's history with the Whitford's. Something buried for a long time."

"The Whitford's." Dean's eyebrows rose. "Arthur Whitford is old money, old power. If your family had dealings with his..."

"SPEAKING OF OLD FAMILIES," Dean said, his tone shifting. "Do you know Peter Grayson? The antiques dealer?"

"HE'S BEEN a regular at my café for years. Why?"

"I was thinking about him on the flight over. His father, Edward—he was quite the character back in the day. Charming as anything, but everyone knew he had a gambling problem." Dean shook his head. "Lost the family fortune at the card tables, or so the story went. By the time he died, there was nothing left but debts and that dusty shop full of antiques." He paused. "Always wondered how Peter managed to turn things around so quickly. One year he was about to close, the next he was renovating the showroom and wearing suits that cost more than my guitar."

"I don't know what they had. That's the problem. I don't know anything." Faye pressed her hands to her temples. "And now someone's dead, and I'm a suspect, and there's a ball tomorrow where I'm supposed to smile and compete in a dessert contest like everything's normal."

Anne reached over and took her hand. "Then that's exactly what you do. You go to the ball. You hold your head high. You don't let them see you sweat."

"And you keep your eyes open," Dean added. "Because whoever did this—they'll be there too. Watching. Waiting. And sometimes the best way to catch a killer is to let them think they've gotten away with it."

Faye looked at her oldest friends, at their familiar faces and their steady certainty, and felt something she hadn't felt in days.

Hope.

8

Before the Storm
SATURDAY, DECEMBER 2OTH.
THE DAY OF THE BALL.

Saturday morning dawned grey and cold, the kind of December day that makes you grateful for warm kitchens and hot coffee. Dixie, welcome back I missed you, as she opened the door to let her in. Would you do me a favor and look after Tiny? With her usual big smile Dixie said "sure thing, Aunt Faye, go do what you need to do" and Faye walked to the harbor.

The Lobsta Shack was quiet this morning, only a few fishermen at the counter nursing cups of coffee and plates of eggs. Yves Brown looked up when she entered, his weathered face broke into a welcoming smile.

"Faye. Sit. Coffee's fresh."

She slid onto a stool at the end of the counter, away from

the other customers. Yves poured her a cup without asking and slid it across the worn wood.

I heard that the Ball is tonight" he said quietly, wiping down the counter in the methodical way of someone who'd done it ten thousand times before. "You competing?"

"Callie let me use her kitchen. The pudding's ready."

Yves nodded slowly. "Good. Don't let them run you out of town, Faye. Some of us know better."

"Thank you." "Yves, can I ask you something?"

"Ask."

"The property sales you mentioned—your cousin's boat repair shop. Do you remember who the buyer was? The company name?"

Yves's eyes narrowed slightly. "Why do you want to know?"

"I think my family might be connected to that purchase. I need to understand."

For a long moment, Yves said nothing. Then he leaned closer, his voice dropping to barely above a whisper.

"Coastal Heritage Holdings. That was the name on the papers. My cousin thought it sounded legitimate—heritage, you know, like they cared about preserving the town." His laugh was bitter. "Turned out it was just a front. One of a dozen companies, all connected, all buying up pieces of Butternut Cove."

"Connected to who?"

"That's the question, isn't it?" Yves straightened, glancing toward the other customers. "I've heard rumors. Names. But nothing I can prove. And the people who tried to prove it..." He met her eyes. "Be careful, Faye. Margaret asked questions too. Look where it got her."

Faye nodded slowly, wrapping her hands around the warm coffee cup. Coastal Heritage Holdings. Another piece of the puzzle. Another thread to follow.

"One more thing," she said. "Do you know anything about Lot 47? A property that was transferred in 1987.

Something flickered in Yves's expression—recognition? Wariness? "Lot 47," he repeated slowly. "That's the old lighthouse keeper's cottage. The one that burned down in '89." He studied her face. "Why do you ask?"

"It belonged to my family once. The Harper Family Trust."

Yves was quiet for a moment. "Your family," he said finally. "And the Whitford's. There's history there, Faye. Old history. The kind people don't talk about anymore." He shook his head. "Ask Arthur. If anyone knows, he does."

Arthur. Who she was meeting this afternoon. Who had promised to tell her about her family's connection to his.

"I will," Faye said. "Thank you, Yves."

She left money on the counter and walked out into the December morning, her mind churning with questions she didn't have answers to.

HOW SWEET *It Is* was bustling when Faye arrived, the Saturday morning crowd lined up for pastries and coffee. Callie spotted her through the crowd and waved her toward the kitchen.

"Your pudding is perfect," Callie announced, beaming. "I steamed it this morning. It is dark and smells so good. It's ready to transport whenever you want to take it."

The figgy pudding sat on the counter, dark and glossy, ready to be placed on its presentation plate. Looking at it, Faye felt a surge of something like defiance. This was her grandmother's recipe. Her heritage. Her place in this town's traditions. No one was going to take that from her.

"Callie, thank you. You saved the day! I'm afraid I can't come back for it this afternoon," Faye said. "I have a meeting with Arthur before the Ball. Would you bring it with your dessert when you come?"

"I'd be happy to do that." Callie gave a reassuring hug and raised an eyebrow. "Any idea what this mysterious meeting is about?"

"Something about my family's history with the Whitford's. And maybe my Board application." Faye shrugged. "Arthur's been hinting at it for days. I suppose I'll finally find out."

"Well, whatever it is, don't let him make you late for the competition." Callie squeezed her arm. "I want to see Kent Blake's face when your pudding wins."

Faye managed a smile. "From your lips to Arthur's taste buds."

Allison appeared from the back, wiping flour from her apron. "Ms. Harper? Good luck tonight. I'll be there—helping serve. If you need anything..."

"Thank you, Allison." Faye said and then to herself silent thank you for these small kindnesses—Callie's kitchen, Yves's coffee, Allison's shy support—they mattered more than anyone probably knew.

She walked home through streets that were slowly coming alive with Ball preparations. Workers strung lights along the lampposts. Someone was testing the sound system at Beacon Hall—she could hear snatches of music floating on the cold air. The town was getting ready for its biggest event of the year, and despite everything, Faye felt the pull of it. The tradition. The community. The magic of a Victorian Christmas in Butternut Cove.

———

SATURDAY AFTERNOON. Two hours before the Ball.

Faye arrived at Beacon Hall in her regular clothes—jeans, a warm sweater, her practical winter coat. The pale blue ball gown hung at home, waiting. She'd change after this meeting, after she finally learned what Arthur had been so eager to tell her.

The Hall was transformed. Workers bustled everywhere, arranging flowers, adjusting lights, draping garlands of fresh greenery along the banisters. The air smelled of pine and beeswax candles. Somewhere in the depths of the building, a string quartet was warming up, fragments of waltzes drifting through the corridors.

Henry Lawson met her at the door, his face drawn and tired, grief etched into every line.

"Faye." He nodded formally. "Mr. Whitford is expecting you."

He led her through the bustling main hall, past the ballroom where tables were being set for the evening, past the sealed door to the archives—still wrapped in yellow crime scene tape—and into a small sitting room at the back of the house.

Arthur Whitford stood by the window, looking out at the grey December afternoon. He turned when she entered, and Faye was struck by how tired he looked. The jolly man who'd spread Christmas cheer through her café just two days ago seemed diminished somehow, as if Margaret's death had stolen something essential from him.

"Faye." He gestured to a chair. "Thank you for coming. Please, sit."

She sat. Henry withdrew, closing the door behind him, and they were alone.

"I owe you an apology," Arthur began, lowering himself into the chair across from her. "I've been mysterious. Hinting at things. Leaving you confused." He sighed. "I'm an old man who thought he had more time than he did."

"Arthur, what is this about?"

He was quiet for a moment, gathering his thoughts. "I wanted to tell you about your family. About the Harpers and the Whitford's. There was a connection, once. A good one.

Your grandmother Bee and my grandmother were close friends. They worked together on the Historical Society, on preserving this town's heritage." He smiled faintly. "Bee was a remarkable woman. You have her spirit."

"Thank you." Faye waited, sensing there was more.

"There was also," Arthur continued carefully, "some business between our families. Properties. Transfers. The details are... complicated. I thought— "He stopped, shook his head. "I thought I might have found something important. Something that would interest you. But with Margaret's death, everything has changed. The archives are sealed. The records I needed are inaccessible."

"What kind of records?"

Arthur's expression became guarded. "I can't say more. Not yet. Not until I'm certain." He leaned forward. "But I want you to know—whatever happened to Margaret, whatever she discovered in those archives—it wasn't your fault. You're not responsible. And I don't believe for a moment that you had anything to do with her death."

"Thank you," Faye said again, though the words felt inadequate.

"As for your Board application." Arthur settled back in his chair. "I'm afraid I have disappointing news. The Historical Society has decided to postpone accepting new members until the investigation is concluded. It's not a reflection on you personally—your application is excellent. But under the circumstances..."

"I understand."

"We'll revisit it in the New Year." Arthur rose, signaling the meeting was ending. "For now, let's focus on tonight. The Ball. The competition." His smile was tired but genuine. "Margaret would have wanted us to carry on. She believed in traditions. In community."

Faye stood as well. "Arthur—at the Ball tonight—you're planning to give a speech?"

Something flickered in his eyes. "Yes. I had planned—" He stopped. "I had planned to make an announcement. But I've reconsidered. Given everything that's happened." He moved toward the door. "I'll announce a memorial instead. A park in Margaret's honor. Something to celebrate her life rather than..." He didn't finish.

As she moved to the door, Faye turned and asked do you think we can do something to hide the crime scene tape across the archive's door?

Thank you, Arthur, replied, I feel as you do and I have taken steps to shield that from public view. Good, I'll see you tonight. Arthur clasped her hand.

Faye didn't press. She'd learned enough—for now.

"I'll see you tonight," she said.

"Yes." Arthur clasped her hand warmly. "And Faye? Be careful. Please. Whatever Margaret knew... it's dangerous. I don't want to see anyone else get hurt."

She walked out of Beacon Hall into the cold December afternoon, her mind full of questions.

———

HOME. One hour until the Ball.

Faye stood before the mirror in her bedroom, the pale blue Victorian silk gown flowing around her like water. Dixie had helped with the buttons—dozens of tiny pearl buttons up the back—and now she hovered behind her, holding a pair of elbow-length gloves.

"You look beautiful, Aunt Faye," Dixie said softly.

"Thank you, sweetheart." Faye turned, examining herself. The gown was a masterpiece of historical accuracy—high neckline, fitted bodice, full skirt that shimmered when she moved. She'd found it at an estate sale two years ago, never imagining she'd actually have an occasion to wear it.

Now here she was. Going to a ball.

"Evan's on his way," Dixie said, checking her phone. "We'll bring Tiny and the others in an hour or so. Jaxson's coming with us from Callie's, and Fig too. Oh, and Ebenezer —we figured out how to get him in the van without too much drama."

Faye smiled despite herself. "The Ball won't know what hit it."

"That's kind of the point." Dixie grinned. "Evan says we'll make an entrance."

Faye knelt to say goodbye to Tiny, stretched along the cushioned nook by the wall, already wearing his gold wreath-style necklace. His nails had been painted gold that morning —Dixie's handiwork—and he looked every inch the regal companion of a Victorian lady.

"I'll see you soon, honey," Faye murmured, stroking the Dane's massive head. "Watch over things here."

Tiny's dark eyes seemed to say: *Don't worry. I always do.*

Faye gathered her cloak, took one last look in the mirror, and stepped out into the December evening.

Beacon Hall awaited. The Ball. The competition. The killer, somewhere among the dancers.

And Faye, walking into danger with her eyes wide open.

9

The Victorian Ball
SATURDAY, DECEMBER 20TH.

Beacon Hall blazed with light.

Every window glowed golden against the December darkness, and the grand entrance was framed by towering arrangements of pine boughs, holly, and winter roses. Luminaries lined the walkway—hundreds of small paper bags weighted with sand, each holding a flickering candle that cast dancing shadows on the fresh dusting of snow. The effect was magical, timeless, as if the building had slipped backward a hundred years to an era of gaslight and horse-drawn carriages.

Faye paused at the entrance, gathering her courage. Her pale blue gown ruffled by the cold breeze, and she pulled her velvet cloak tighter around her shoulders. Somewhere inside, a string quartet was playing—she recognized the opening strains of a Strauss waltz—and the murmur of voices and laughter drifted out into the night.

She could do this. She *would* do this.

The doors opened, and she stepped into another world.

———

THE GRAND FOYER had been transformed. Garlands of fresh greenery wound around the banisters and doorframes, studded with red berries and gilded pinecones. A massive Christmas tree dominated the space, its branches heavy with Victorian ornaments—glass balls, delicate angels, strands of tinsel that caught the light from dozens of candles. The air smelled of pine and cinnamon and the warm vanilla scent of beeswax.

And everywhere—*everywhere*—there were people. Ladies in elaborate gowns of silk and velvet, gentlemen in tailcoats and cravats, children darting between the adults in their own miniature Victorian finery. The Historical Society had outdone itself. This wasn't just a party; it was a living tableau, a window into Butternut Cove's past.

Faye ascended the McIntyre stairway, elegant and expansive and handed her cloak to an attendant and moved into the crowd, acutely aware of the eyes that followed her. Some curious. Some cold. A few openly hostile.

She lifted her chin and kept walking.

"Faye!"

Tessa emerged from the crowd, resplendent in deep burgundy, her dark hair piled high in an elaborate Victorian style. She seized Faye's hands and squeezed them tightly.

"You came. I wasn't sure you would."

"Wild horses couldn't keep me away." Faye managed a smile. "Besides, I have a pudding to defend."

"That's the spirit." Tessa linked her arm through Faye's.

"Come on. Let me show you where they've set up the competition."

———

THE DESSERT COMPETITION had been given pride of place in the ballroom, on a damask-draped table beneath an enormous crystal chandelier. Around the focal display, more than two dozen other entries crowded the table—tarts and trifles, layered cakes, cookies stacked in careful towers—all waiting their turn to be noticed.

Two puddings sat side by side on silver pedestals, each with a small placard identifying its creator.

Faye's was darker, more compact, glistening with the brandy glaze her grandmother had taught her to brush on while the pudding was still warm. Kent's was larger, paler, decorated with an elaborate arrangement of candied fruits and sugared rosemary.

"They're so different," Tessa observed. "Yours looks traditional. His looks... showy."

"Presentation versus substance." Faye studied the two puddings. "Arthur will judge on taste, though. At least, that's the tradition."

"Speaking of Kent..."

Faye followed Tessa's gaze across the ballroom. Kent Blake stood near the refreshment table, resplendent in a perfectly tailored Victorian suit, his silver hair gleaming under the candlelight. He was holding court with a small group of admirers, his laugh carrying across the room—too loud, too confident, the laugh of a man who expected to win.

As if sensing her attention, Kent turned. Their eyes met. He raised his champagne glass in a mocking salute.

Faye didn't look away. She held his gaze until he was the one who turned back to his admirers, something flickering in his expression that might have been annoyance.

"Well," Tessa said dryly, "that was subtle."

"He started it."

"Very mature, both of you." But Tessa was smiling. "Come on. Let's find you some champagne before the speeches start."

━━━

THE NEXT HOUR passed in a blur of introductions, small talk, and careful navigation. Faye circulated through the crowd, champagne in hand, playing the role expected of her: gracious guest, eager competitor, innocent citizen with nothing to hide.

It was exhausting.

Charlotte Whitford held court near the fireplace, elegant in dove-gray silk, Oliver a silent presence at her side. When Faye approached to pay her respects, Charlotte's smile was cool and correct.

"Faye. How brave of you to come."

"I wouldn't miss the Ball, Mrs. Whitford. It's a wonderful tradition."

"Indeed." Charlotte's gaze swept over Faye's gown with the practiced assessment of someone who could price every stitch. "Such a shame about Margaret. She so loved these events."

"She did." Faye kept her voice steady. "She'll be missed."

"Will she?" Something flickered behind Charlotte's eyes—something hard and knowing. "Margaret had a talent for... uncovering things. Not always a welcome talent."

Oliver shifted beside his wife, his hand coming to rest on her elbow. A warning? A comfort? Faye couldn't tell.

"If you'll excuse us," Charlotte said, already turning away. "We should circulate."

They moved off into the crowd, Charlotte's silk gown whispering against the polished floor. Faye watched them go,

Charlotte's words echoing in her mind: *A talent for uncovering things. Not always a welcome talent.*

A threat? A confession? Or simply the observation of a woman who'd lived long enough to know that some secrets were better left buried?

"FAYE."

The voice came from behind her, smooth and cultured. Faye turned to find Peter Grayson approaching, impeccable in his Victorian evening attire, a glass of whiskey in his hand.

"Mr. Grayson." She kept her tone neutral.

"I wanted to offer my condolences." Peter's expression was appropriately somber. "About your café, I mean. Terrible business, having it closed during the Christmas season. I imagine it's quite a hardship."

"It's inconvenient," Faye agreed carefully. "But I expect it will reopen soon."

"Of course, of course." Peter sipped his whiskey. "And the investigation? Any progress? I imagine you must be eager to clear your name."

There was something beneath his words—something probing, testing. Faye remembered what Dean had said: *Follow the money.* She remembered the initials in Margaret's notebook: P.G.

"I'm confident the truth will come out," she said. "It always does."

Peter's smile didn't waver, but something shifted in his eyes —a flicker of calculation, quickly hidden. "Indeed it does. Well..." He raised his glass in a small toast. "Best of luck with the competition. I hear Kent's quite confident this year."

"Confidence isn't everything."

"No," Peter agreed, something cold beneath his pleasant tone. "No, it isn't."

As Peter disappeared into the crowd, Faye moved toward the refreshment table—and nearly collided with him again near the service corridor. She moved away out of his sight but close enough to overhear the conversation. He had his phone pressed to his ear, his back half-turned, his voice low and urgent.

"I told you, I need more time. The money will be there, I just—" He paused, listening. "No. No, that's not acceptable. You can't just—" Another pause, longer this time. His shoulders stiffened. "Fine. Fine. But after this, we're done. You hear me? Done."

He ended the call with a sharp gesture and stood for a moment, composing himself. Then he straightened his cuffs, fixed a smile on his face, and walked back toward the ballroom as if nothing had happened.

Money troubles. Faye filed that away. But plenty of people had money troubles—it didn't make them murderers.

He moved away, disappearing into the crowd, and Faye released a breath she hadn't realized she'd been holding.

━━

ROSE FAIRWEATHER STOOD ALONE near the windows, her emerald gown a vivid splash of color against the winter darkness beyond the glass. She was staring out at nothing, her champagne untouched, and when Faye approached, she startled visibly.

"Oh! Faye. You surprised me."

"I'm sorry. I didn't mean to startle you. Faye paused. "Are you alright?"

Rose replied in disbelief, "Am I all right? My colleague is dead, the archives are a crime scene, and everyone's pretending everything's normal because—" She stopped, pressed a hand across her throat. "I'm sorry. That was inappropriate."

"No. It's honest." Faye moved to stand beside her, both of them looking out at the night. "This must be difficult for you. Working with Margaret every day, and now..."

"She was brilliant, you know." Rose's voice was soft. "Absolutely brilliant at research. She could find connections no one else saw. Patterns in the records that seemed random until she explained them." Rose paused. "I think that's what got her killed. Seeing too much. Understanding too much."

"What do you think she understood?"

Rose turned to look at Faye, and for a moment, Faye saw something in her eyes—fear, guilt, indecision—before it was masked behind professional composure.

"I don't know," Rose said. But the way she said it—too quickly, too firmly—made Faye look at her more closely.

"Rose." Faye kept her voice gentle. "If there's something you're not telling me—"

"It's nothing." Rose's hand went to her throat, where a delicate gold chain glinted. "It's just—I've been so worried. About my own situation, I mean. Not about Margaret." She took a shaky breath. "I have debts. Stupid debts—credit cards, a car I couldn't afford, clothes I bought to fit in with people like Charlotte." She smiled ruefully. "I grew up with nothing, you know. And when I finally got this job, surrounded by all these wealthy families and their beautiful things, I wanted so badly to belong. To look like I belonged."

Understanding dawned. Rose's designer clothes. Her careful grooming. The way she always seemed slightly over-dressed for Butternut Cove.

"That's why you've been so nervous," Faye said quietly. "You're afraid people will find out."

"Margaret knew." Rose's eyes glistened. "She found some of my creditor notices in the archives—I'd hidden them there, stupid, I know. She was kind about it. Said everyone makes mistakes." She wiped away a stray tear. "But I keep thinking —if people knew I was in debt, if they knew I'd been hiding things—they might think I had something to do with what happened to her. That I was protecting some financial secret."

"I would never hurt Margaret. I admired her. I just—I'm so ashamed of my own foolishness, and I've been terrified that it would all come out in the investigation."

Faye studied her face—the genuine distress, the embarrassment, the relief of finally confessing. Whatever Rose was hiding, it wasn't murder. Just human weakness. The desperate need to belong.

"I won't tell anyone," Faye said. "Your debts are your business. But Rose—"

Faye studied Rose's face—the careful composure cracking to reveal the frightened woman beneath—and felt an unexpected kinship. How many times had she worn that same mask? How many times had she said *I'm fine* when everything was falling apart?

"I understand," Faye said quietly. "More than you know."

Before Faye could press further, a commotion near the entrance drew their attention. Rose seized the distraction gratefully.

"I should find Beatrice Larkspur, I need to give her an update from the research she asked for. She touched Faye's arm briefly. "Be careful, Faye. Please. Thank you. Thank you for listening and for understanding."

She slipped away into the crowd, leaving Faye with more questions than answers.

⊏⊐

FAYE FOUND Henry Lawson in a quiet corner near the library, away from the noise and glitter of the main celebration. He sat alone on a velvet settee, a glass of untouched punch beside him, staring at nothing.

He looked up when she approached, and Faye's heart

clenched at what she saw in his face. This wasn't the grief of a colleague. This was something deeper, more devastating.

"Henry." She sat beside him, uninvited but somehow certain he needed company. "I'm so sorry about Margaret."

Henry's took a slow deep breath before he replied. "Everyone's sorry. Everyone says what a loss it is, what a tragedy." He shook his head. "They didn't know her. Not really. Not the way..."

He stopped, unable to finish.

"The way you did?" Faye asked gently.

Henry was quiet for a long moment. When he spoke, his voice was barely above a whisper.

"Twenty years. I worked beside her for twenty years. Every day, watching her light up when she found something interesting in the archives. Listening to her talk about history like it was alive, like the people in those old documents were friends she was catching up with." His hands trembled around the glass. "I never told her. Never said a word. And now..."

Faye reached out and covered his hand with hers. "I think she knew, Henry. I think she must have known."

"Did she?" Hope flickered in his eyes, painful to see. "Do you really think so?"

"I do." Faye anticipated this was possible but at the moment it was a kind comment, she was able to give kindness freely and hoped it would help him feel more settled.

Henry nodded slowly, some of the tension easing from his shoulders. "Thank you, Faye. That... that helps."

A gong sounded from the ballroom—the signal that the speeches were about to begin.

"We should go," Faye said, rising. "Arthur will be speaking soon."

Henry stood, straightening his coat, pulling himself together with visible effort. "Yes. Yes, of course. The show must go on." His smile was sad. "That's what Margaret would have said."

THE BALLROOM FELL silent as Arthur Whitford took his place at the podium, a spotlight catching the silver in his hair and the gleam of his watch chain. His voice, when he spoke, was steady and strong.

"Friends. Neighbors. Fellow citizens of Butternut Cove." Arthur's gaze swept across the crowd. "We gather tonight to celebrate a tradition that stretches back over a century—the Victorian Christmas Ball, a reminder of who we are and where we came from."

Applause rippled through the room. Arthur waited for it to subside.

"But this year, our celebration is touched by sorrow. Two days ago, we lost a beloved member of our community. Margaret Ellis dedicated her life to preserving our history, to ensuring that the stories of Butternut Cove would never be forgotten." His voice wavered slightly. "She was my colleague, my friend, and her loss diminishes us all."

The room was utterly silent now. Faye saw handkerchiefs dabbing at eyes, saw Henry Lawson bow his head, saw Charlotte Whitford's expression carefully, perfectly blank.

"In Margaret's honor," Arthur continued, "I am announcing tonight the creation of the Margaret Ellis Memorial Park. It will be built on the waterfront, on land donated by the Historical Society, and it will include a garden dedicated to her memory." He paused. "A place of peace. A place of reflection. A place where future generations can remember a woman who loved this town with her whole heart."

More applause—warmer now, genuine. Arthur smiled, but Faye noticed the slight tremor in his fingers.

This wasn't what he'd planned to announce. She was certain of it. Whatever revelation he'd been building toward—whatever truth Margaret had uncovered—he'd buried it. Replaced it with something safe.

"And now," Arthur said, his tone lightening, "to the matter you've all been waiting for. The annual dessert competition!"

Laughter and cheers. The mood shifted, the shadow of death giving way to the warmth of tradition. Arthur gestured toward the competition table, where Faye's and Kent's puddings waited under the chandelier's glow.

"This year, we have two exceptional entries. From Kent Blake of *Simply I Do*, a pudding in the French tradition— elegant, refined, a testament to culinary artistry." Arthur nodded toward Kent, who preened visibly. "And from Faye Harper of *The Heirloom Table Café*, a pudding made from her grandmother's recipe—traditional, heartfelt, a taste of Christmas past."

Faye felt the weight of hundreds of eyes on her. She smiled, hoping it looked more confident than she felt.

"As is tradition," Arthur continued, "I have already tasted both puddings in a private judging before the Ball. The winner will be announced shortly, but first—" He spread his arms wide. "—let us dance! Let us celebrate! Let us honor Margaret's memory by living fully, as she would have wanted!"

The string quartet struck up a waltz, and couples began moving toward the dance floor. Arthur stepped away from the podium, mopping his brow with a handkerchief, and was immediately surrounded by well-wishers.

Faye watched him from across the room, questions burning in her mind. What had he originally planned to say? What truth was too dangerous to speak?

And why did she have the terrible feeling that the danger wasn't over—that it was, in fact, just beginning?

THE QUARTET YIELDED the stage to Dean and Anne, who took their places with the easy confidence of seasoned performers. Dean had traded his Victorian coat for something with more movement—still period-appropriate, but practical for a musician—and Anne settled behind the piano that had been rolled out for their set.

"Good evening, Butternut Cove," Dean said into the microphone, his Nashville drawl warming the words. "We're so honored to be here tonight, celebrating this beautiful tradition with all of you."

He caught Faye's eye across the room and winked. She felt some of her tension ease. Whatever else happened tonight, she had friends here. People who believed in her.

Dean launched into a medley of Christmas carols—traditional ones, arranged in his signature style, acoustic guitar blending with Anne's piano. *God Rest Ye Merry Gentlemen* flowed into *O Come All Ye Faithful*, then a hauntingly beautiful version of *In the Bleak Midwinter* that brought tears to more than a few eyes.

Faye found herself swaying to the music, momentarily lost in the beauty of it. The candlelight, the garlands, the smell of pine and cinnamon—for just a moment, she could pretend that everything was normal. That Margaret wasn't dead. That a killer wasn't walking among them.

I'm fine, she thought automatically—and then stopped. No. She wasn't fine. A woman was dead. Someone in this glittering room might be her killer. And Faye was standing here in a vintage dress, pretending to belong to a world that might be rotten at its core.

But she was still standing. Still fighting. That had to count for something.

Then she saw Kent Blake slip away from the crowd, moving toward the competition table with a studied casualness that immediately raised her suspicions.

She watched, hidden behind a pillar, as Kent glanced around to make sure no one was looking. Then, with the quick precision of someone who'd planned this moment, he lifted the dome covering Faye's pudding, produced a small knife from his pocket, and cut away a slice.

Faye's blood boiled. The *nerve*. The absolute *gall*.

She started forward, ready to confront him, but something stopped her. Kent wasn't eating the slice. He was wrapping it in a napkin, hiding it in his pocket. And the knife—he was looking around for somewhere to stash it, finally shoving it beneath the damask tablecloth.

This wasn't sabotage. This was a prank. A petty, childish prank designed to make her pudding look incomplete when the judging was announced.

She should report him. She should march over there right now and expose his cheating to everyone.

But something held her back. A whisper of instinct, perhaps. Or the memory of Dean's words: *Sometimes the best way to catch someone is to let them think they've gotten away with it.*

She filed the information away and retreated to the shadows, watching Kent return to the crowd with a satisfied smirk on his face.

Later. She would deal with him later.

For now, there were bigger concerns. She'd seen the way Arthur looked during his speech—the fear behind his eyes, the relief when the dangerous moment passed. Someone in this room had killed Margaret. Someone in this room might try again.

And Faye intended to find out who.

———

THE COMMOTION at the entrance announced their arrival before Faye could see them.

Heads turned. Whispers rippled through the crowd. And then the ballroom doors swung open to reveal a sight that made Faye's heart swell with equal parts love and exasperation.

Dixie came first with Fig on her shoulder, looking older than her years in a borrowed Victorian dress, her chin held high. Fig surveyed the ballroom with the regal disdain of a feline empress, her blue eyes missing nothing.

Beside Dixie walked Evan Doyle, scrubbed and uncomfortable in what was clearly his father's old suit, but managing to carry himself with quiet dignity.

And behind them, Tiny led the procession, magnificent in his gold wreath collar, his painted nails gleaming. He moved with the stately grace of a creature who knew exactly how impressive he looked. Jaxson trotted beside him, his golden fur brushed to a shine, pink tongue lolling in a happy grin and his reindeer antlers securely affixed to his head. And bringing up the rear, waddling with surprising dignity, came Ebenezer. Someone—Dixie, surely—had tied a small red bow around his neck and a cap on his head. He honked softly as he entered, as if announcing his own arrival.

The crowd parted before them like the Red Sea, half-scandalized and half-charmed. Faye saw Arthur Whitford throw back his head and laugh—a genuine laugh, the first she'd heard from him all evening.

"Aunt Faye!" Dixie spotted her and waved. "We made it!"

Faye hurried to meet them, kneeling to greet Tiny, who pressed his massive head against Faye's chest in wordless reunion. The Dane's tail wagged slowly, his dark eyes saying: I'm here now. Everything will be all right.

"You're impossible," Faye murmured, but she was smiling. "All of you. Completely impossible."

"We thought you might need backup," Evan said quietly, a shy smile crossing his face. "Dixie's idea."

"It was a team effort," Dixie corrected. "And anyway, look at them. They were born for this."

She wasn't wrong. Tiny had already attracted a circle of admirers, accepting their attention with gracious patience. Jaxson was making friends with everyone who offered a pat.

Even Ebenezer seemed to be enjoying himself, honking conversationally at anyone who came too close.

Only Fig remained aloof, watching the proceedings from Dixie's shoulder with an expression that suggested she was cataloging everyone's secrets.

Faye straightened, looking around the ballroom at the glittering crowd, the candlelight, the Christmas splendor. Her friends were here. Her family—her strange, wonderful, eclectic family—was here.

Whatever came next, she wouldn't face it alone.

The string quartet began another waltz. Somewhere in the crowd, Arthur Whitford was accepting congratulations on his memorial announcement. Somewhere else, Kent Blake was nursing his secret sabotage. And somewhere—Faye was anxious—afraid a killer was watching, waiting, planning their next move.

The Ball was only just beginning.

10

The Rescue

SATURDAY, DECEMBER 20TH.
THE GONG SOUNDED AGAIN,

...cutting through the music and chatter.

"Ladies and gentlemen!" Arthur Whitford stood at the podium once more, his face flushed with the warmth of the room and perhaps one too many glasses of champagne. "The moment you've all been waiting for. The results of our annual dessert competition!"

The crowd gathered around, a sea of Victorian finery pressing toward the stage. Faye found herself near the front, Tessa on one side and Tiny pressed against her leg on the other. The Dane's body was tense, his ears pricked forward, as if he sensed something Faye couldn't.

Across the room, Fig sat upright on Dixie's shoulder, her blue eyes fixed on the podium with unusual intensity. Jaxson had stopped his friendly wandering and stood at attention beside Callie. Even Ebenezer, who had been contentedly investigating the hors d'oeuvres table, went still.

Something was wrong. Faye could feel it—a tension in the air that had nothing to do with competition nerves.

"As you know," Arthur continued, "I tasted both puddings earlier this evening in a blind judging. Both were exceptional —truly exceptional. Kent's interpretation brought French sophistication to a British classic, while Faye's honored the traditional recipes that make this dessert so beloved."

He paused for effect, and Faye saw Kent Blake lean forward, his face tight with anticipation.

"But in the end, there can be only one winner." Arthur smiled. "And this year, the winner is... Faye Harper, for her grandmother's figgy pudding!"

Applause erupted around her. Tessa squeezed her arm, beaming. Someone pushed her gently toward the podium, and Faye found herself walking forward in a daze, accepting Arthur's warm handshake and the small crystal trophy he pressed into her hands.

"Speech!" someone called from the crowd.

Faye looked out at the sea of faces—some friendly, some not—and felt her throat tighten. "I... thank you. This recipe belonged to my grandmother, and her mother before her. To share it with Butternut Cove means more than I can say."

She caught Callie's eye in the crowd.

"And thank you to Callie Sweet, who opened her kitchen when I needed it most. This win belongs to both of us."

The crowd applauded, but Faye's heart was steady and calm now. They had worked creatively, modernized what needed changing, and in the end—she was proud of what they'd made.

More applause. Faye stepped back from the podium, clutching the trophy, and allowed herself a moment of pure, uncomplicated joy.

Jenny would have loved this. The thought came unbidden, sharp and sweet. Her daughter had always cheered the loudest at every small victory—a good grade, a successful recipe, a compliment from a stranger. *Mom, you're amazing,* she used to say, with all the fierce conviction of childhood.

Faye blinked back the sting in her eyes. For once, she didn't push the memory away. She let it sit beside the joy, two truths existing together.

It lasted exactly three seconds.

Because that's when she saw Kent Blake's face—not disappointed, as she'd expected, but smug. Satisfied. The face of a man who had a secret.

And that's when Fig began to yowl.

<hr />

THE SOUND CUT through the celebration like a knife—a high, urgent cry that was nothing like the Siamese's usual imperious meows. Heads turned. Conversations died.

Fig was standing now, her fur bristled, her tail puffed to twice its normal size. Her blue eyes were fixed on something across the room, and she yowled again—a sound of pure, primal warning.

"What on earth—" Dixie began, but she never finished.

Because Fig launched herself from Dixie's shoulder and streaked across the ballroom floor like a cream-colored missile. Jaxson bolted after her, barking. Ebenezer spread his wings and honked—a sound so loud and alarming that several guests stumbled backward in shock.

And Tiny—Tiny, who never left Faye's side without permission—pulled free and ran, ears flat, body suddenly all focus.

"Tiny!" Faye dropped the trophy and followed, pushing through the crowd, her heart pounding. What was happening? What had they seen?

The animals converged on the refreshment area, where servers in Victorian dress were preparing plates of dessert. In the center of the chaos stood Allison Day, frozen in place, holding a china plate with a generous slice of figgy pudding.

She was walking toward Arthur Whitford.

Fig reached her first, weaving between Allison's ankles with a cry that made the young woman stumble. Jaxson circled, barking frantically. Ebenezer honked and honked, his wings spread wide, blocking Allison's path to Arthur.

And then Tiny arrived.

One hundred and forty pounds of Dane, moving at full speed, collided with Allison Day's hip. The impact wasn't brutal, only precise—but it was enough. Allison cried out, her arms pinwheeling, and the plate flew from her hands.

The figgy pudding sailed through the air in a graceful arc, trailing crumbs and brandy sauce, before landing with a spectacular splatter on the polished floor.

Silence.

Absolute, shocked silence.

Then Arthur Whitford stepped forward, his face ashen. He bent slowly, stiffly, and picked up a fragment of the ruined dessert. He raised it to his nose.

And went very, very still.

"Almonds," he said, his voice barely above a whisper. "This smells of almonds."

Faye felt the blood drain from her face. Almonds. The distinctive bitter-sweet scent that could mask something far more deadly. The same scent that had been found on the cookies beside Margaret's body.

Arthur looked up, and his eyes—terrified, knowing—met Faye's across the ruined dessert.

"Someone," he said, "just tried to kill me."

PANDEMONIUM.

The word barely captured it. Screams erupted. Guests surged toward the exits. Someone knocked over a candelabra, sending flames licking across a tablecloth until a quick-thinking server doused it with champagne. Officers that Luke had stationed around the perimeter pushed through the crowd, trying to restore order.

Faye fought her way to Arthur's side, Tiny close behind. The old man was trembling, one hand pressed to his chest, but his eyes were sharp and alert.

"Arthur—are you all right?"

"I didn't eat it." His voice shook. "Thanks to your remarkable dog and your collection of pets, I didn't eat it." He looked at Tiny with something like wonder. "How did he know? How did they all know starting with the cat?"

Faye didn't have an answer. She knelt beside Tiny, wrapping her arms around the Dane's neck. Tiny's heart was racing beneath his fur, but his eyes were calm—the eyes of a creature who had done what needed to be done.

"Good boy," Faye whispered. "Good, brave dog."

Across the room, Allison Day had collapsed against a pillar, sobbing. Callie was with her, an arm around her shoulders, speaking in low, soothing tones. Dixie and Evan had gathered Jaxson and Fig, keeping them calm amid the chaos. Ebenezer had stationed himself near Arthur like a feathered bodyguard, honking at anyone who came too close.

Luke appeared at Faye's elbow, his face grim. "What happened?"

"Someone poisoned a slice of my pudding." Faye pointed to the mess on the floor. "The same way they poisoned my cookies that killed Margaret. Bitter almond scent—you can smell it."

Luke crouched, sniffed, and his expression darkened. No almond—not everyone could detect it.

Of the small circle of onlookers, a lucky few could detect it instantly — that faint, bitter scent that meant danger.

Luke, unfortunately, wasn't one of them.

He immediately pulled out his radio and barked orders— seal the exits, preserve the evidence, get a forensics team here now.

"The girl who was serving," he said, straightening. "I need to talk to her. What is her name?"

Faye replied "Allison and she didn't know." Faye was certain of it. She'd seen Allison's face when the pudding flew —confusion, not guilt. Horror, not calculation. "Someone gave her that plate. Someone used her."

"I still need to talk to her." Luke's voice was gentle but firm. "I need to talk to everyone who touched that dessert. Everyone who had access to the serving area."

He moved toward Allison, and Faye let him go. There was nothing she could do for the girl now except hope that Luke saw what she had seen—an innocent person caught in someone else's murderous scheme.

———

FAYE FOUND Allison twenty minutes later, sitting alone in a small anteroom off the main hall. The girl's face was blotchy from crying, her elegant Victorian dress rumpled, her hands twisting in her lap.

"I didn't know," Allison said before Faye could speak. "I swear, Faye, I didn't know. Someone—someone gave me that plate from the kitchen. Said it was for Mr. Whitford. A special serving. I thought—" Her voice broke. "I thought I was just doing my job."

Faye sat beside her. "I believe you, Allison."

"I almost killed him." The words came out in a horrified whisper. "If your dog and the other pets hadn't—if they hadn't stopped me—"

"But he did. Arthur is fine. You're fine." Faye took the girl's cold hands in hers. "This isn't your fault. Someone used you, the same way they used my bakery box and cookie to frame me. We're both victims here."

Allison looked up, hope flickering through her tears. "Do you really think so?"

"I know so." Faye squeezed her hands. "Now think. Who gave you that plate? Did you see their face?"

Allison frowned and thought carefully.

"It was... it was so busy. Everyone was moving around. Someone in a server's uniform, I think. They said—it was a special request from Mrs. Whitford. For her husband."

Faye went very still. Arthur had never been married. She filed that away.

"Was it a man or a woman? Tall or short? Any detail you remember?"

"I..." Allison closed her eyes, concentrating. "Gloves. They were wearing white gloves. When they handed over the plate I looked down so that I would not drop it. I never saw their face, they spoke and I think it was a man." She opened her eyes, anguished. "I'm sorry. I'm so sorry. I should have paid more attention."

"You had no reason to suspect anything." Faye patted her hands and stood. "Tell Grayson everything you told me. He'll understand."

She left Allison in the anteroom and went to find answers of her own.

———

THE COMPETITION TABLE had become a crime scene.

Officers in latex gloves were photographing everything— the two figgy puddings (one now missing a slice, Faye noted grimly), the silver pedestals, the damask cloth. Yellow evidence markers dotted the area like strange flowers.

Faye approached carefully, staying behind the tape, and watched as a young officer lifted the edge of the tablecloth.

"!" The officer's voice was sharp with discovery. "There's something under here."

Luke strode over, and Faye edged closer, craning to see. The officer reached beneath the cloth with gloved hands and withdrew a knife—small, sharp, the kind used for precise cuts. The blade gleamed under the chandelier light, sticky with remnants of dark pudding.

"Bag it," Luke ordered. "We'll check for prints."

Faye thought of Kent Blake, his smug smile, the slice he'd cut from her pudding and hidden in his pocket. His fingerprints would be all over that knife.

She should tell Luke. She should explain what she'd witnessed.

But something held her back. Kent was guilty of sabotage, yes. Petty jealousy and cheating. But murder? She'd seen his face when Arthur announced the almond scent—genuine shock, not the careful blankness of a guilty man.

Still. The knife. His fingerprints. The connection would be made soon enough.

As if summoned by her thoughts, a commotion erupted near the entrance. She turned to see two officers escorting Kent Blake toward Luke, his face pale, his earlier smugness completely gone.

"What is the meaning of this?" Kent sputtered. "I demand to know—"

"Mr. Blake." Luke's voice was cold. "We found a knife under the competition table. Hidden beneath the cloth. Someone suggested it was yours. I have reason to believe it may be connected to tonight's attempted poisoning."

Kent's face went from pale to ashen. "Poisoning? I don't know anything about any poisoning! I just—"

He stopped, realizing too late where his words were leading.

"You just what, Kent?" Luke stepped closer. "The knife appears to have been used to cut a slice of pudding. Faye's pudding, specifically. And we'll be testing it for fingerprints."

The silence stretched. Kent's Adam's apple bobbed. Around them, the remaining guests watched with avid interest, sensing drama.

"It was a prank," Kent finally said, the words coming out in a defeated rush. "Just a stupid prank. I cut a slice from her pudding so it would look tampered with when the winner was announced. I wanted to embarrass her, make people question whether she'd done something to enhance herself." He ran a hand through his silver hair, destroying its careful styling. "I had nothing to do with any poisoning. I swear it."

Luke studied him for a long moment. "You're admitting to tampering with evidence in what is now a criminal investigation."

"It wasn't evidence when I did it! It was just... just a figgy pudding!" Kent's voice cracked. "I didn't know someone was going to try to murder Arthur!"

"We'll need a full statement." Luke nodded to the officers. "Take Mr. Blake to the station. And Kent?" He waited until Kent met his eyes. "I'd suggest cooperating fully. Things will go easier for you if you do."

They led Kent away, and Faye watched him go with a complicated mix of emotions. He'd tried to humiliate her. He'd sabotaged the competition. He'd let his petty jealousy override his better judgment.

But he wasn't the killer. She was certain of it.

Which meant the real killer was still here. Still watching. Still planning.

———

FAYE FOUND Arthur in the small sitting room where they'd met that afternoon—a lifetime ago, it seemed now. He sat in the same chair, but everything else had changed. His face was grey, his hands shaking despite the brandy someone had pressed into them.

"May I?" Faye gestured to the chair across from him.

Arthur nodded wearily. "Please."

She sat, and for a moment, neither of them spoke. The sounds of the disrupted Ball filtered through the walls—voices, footsteps, the occasional honk of Ebenezer still guarding his post by the front door.

"I should have said something," Arthur finally said. "At the speech. I should have told them everything Margaret discovered. Exposed the whole rotten scheme." He shook his head. "Instead, I took the coward's path. Announced a memorial park and pretended everything was fine."

"You were trying to protect yourself."

"Was I?" Arthur's laugh was bitter. "And look how well that worked. They tried to kill me anyway." He took a long slow swallow of brandy. "They'll try again, you know. Now that they know I know. Now that they've shown their hand."

"Then tell Luke. Tell him everything. Let the police protect you."

Arthur looked at her, and she saw something in his eyes—fear, yes, but also a strange kind of resignation.

"It's not that simple, Faye. The people involved... they have influence. Power. The kind of power that can make problems disappear." He set down his glass. "Including old men who ask too many questions."

"Who, Arthur?" Faye leaned forward. "Who is behind this?"

For a moment, she thought he might tell her. His mouth opened, shaped the beginning of a word—

Then Charlotte Whitford swept into the room, Oliver a silent shadow behind her.

"Arthur, darling." Charlotte's voice was smooth,

concerned, perfectly calibrated. "The car is ready. We should get you home. You've had a terrible shock."

Arthur's expression shuttered. Whatever he'd been about to say retreated behind a mask of exhaustion.

"Yes," he said. "Yes, of course. You're right."

He rose, steadying himself on the arm of the chair. Charlotte moved to his side, solicitous, attentive—the perfect picture of a concerned niece.

But as she guided Arthur toward the door, Charlotte's eyes met Faye's. And in them, Faye saw something cold. Something calculating.

A warning.

"Goodnight, Faye," Charlotte said. "Do give my regards to your... menagerie."

They swept out, leaving Faye alone with her racing thoughts.

⸺

THE BALL WAS OVER.

Not officially—the police were still processing the scene, still taking statements—but the magic had fled. Guests trickled out in subdued groups, their Victorian finery somehow diminished, their faces shadowed with unease. The Christmas decorations that had seemed so festive now looked garish, inappropriate. How could you celebrate when a killer walked among you?

Faye found her people gathered near the entrance—Tessa, Dixie, Evan, Callie. And the animals, of course. Always the animals.

She knelt on the cold floor, heedless of her gown, and gathered Tiny into her arms. The Dane submitted to the embrace with patient grace, his tail wagging slowly.

"You saved him," Faye whispered. "You all saved him."

Fig, perched on Dixie's shoulder, made a small sound that

might have been acknowledgment. Jaxson pressed his golden head against Faye's side. Ebenezer honked softly—almost gently—from his position near Evan's feet.

"How did they know?" Dixie asked, her young face troubled. "I mean, Fig just started yowling, and then they all went crazy. Like they could sense something."

"Animals perceive things we can't," Callie said. "Smells, sounds, changes in the air. Fig especially—she's always been sensitive." She reached out and stroked the Siamese's cream-colored fur. "Isn't that right, your majesty?"

Fig blinked slowly, accepting the tribute as her due.

"Whatever the explanation," Tessa said firmly, "Arthur Whitford is alive because of these four. And that's what matters."

Faye stood, brushing off her gown. "Let's go home. All of us. I think we've had enough excitement for one night."

They made their way out into the December darkness, a strange procession—two women in rumpled Victorian gowns, two teenagers in borrowed finery, and four animals who had just prevented a murder.

The luminarias still flickered along the walkway, but their warmth seemed hollow now. Somewhere in Butternut Cove, a killer was nursing their failed plan. Somewhere, they were already plotting their next move.

Faye looked back at Beacon Hall, its windows still blazing with light, and made a silent promise.

I will find you, she thought. *I don't know how yet, but I will find you. And when I do, you'll answer for Margaret. For Arthur. For all of it.*

Tiny pressed against her leg, warm and solid and real.

Tomorrow, the investigation would begin in earnest. Tomorrow, she would look at Margaret's notebook with fresh eyes. Tomorrow, she would find the truth.

But tonight—tonight, she would hold her family close and be grateful they were all still alive.

She thought of Margaret's terrified face in the café, the

way she'd clutched that notebook like a lifeline. *Be careful who you trust.*

Margaret had trusted her. Had chosen her, out of everyone in Butternut Cove, to carry this burden. Faye didn't fully understand why—but she understood obligation. She understood what it meant to be the one left behind, holding the pieces of someone else's unfinished story.

She wouldn't let Margaret down. Whatever it cost her.

11

The Morning After
SUNDAY, DECEMBER 21ST.

Faye woke to grey light filtering through her curtains and the weight of Tiny's head on her feet. For one blissful moment, she didn't remember. Then it all came flooding back—the Ball, the poisoned pudding, the animals' desperate rescue, Charlotte's cold eyes—and she pulled the covers over her head like a child hiding from monsters.

Tiny shifted, his tail thumping against the mattress. A question: Are we getting up?

"I suppose we must," Faye muttered.

She found Dixie already in the kitchen, making coffee with the careful concentration of someone who had taught herself from YouTube videos. Ebenezer honked a greeting from his crate on the back porch, and through the window, Faye could see the December morning—overcast, still, the kind of day that felt suspended between storms.

"You're up early," Faye said.

"Couldn't sleep." Dixie poured two cups and slid one across the counter. "Kept thinking about last night. About what would have happened if Fig hadn't..." She shook her head. "It's scary, Aunt Faye. Someone in this town is a murderer."

"I know, sweetheart." Faye wrapped her hands around the warm mug. "But we're safe. The police are investigating. And our furry guardians are on high alert."

As if to prove her point, Tiny padded into the kitchen and stationed himself by the back door, his dark eyes scanning the yard with professional vigilance.

"I'm going to Evan's later," Dixie said. "His uncle Yves invited us for lunch. Is that okay?"

"Of course." Faye managed a smile. "Just be careful. Stay together. And text me when you get there."

After Dixie left to shower, Faye sat alone at the kitchen table, her coffee growing cold. Her eyes drifted to the drawer where she'd hidden Margaret's notebook—still there, still waiting, still a moral weight she hadn't resolved.

She should tell Luke. She knew she should. But every time she thought about handing it over, something stopped her. Margaret had trusted *her* with this. Margaret had said *don't tell anyone*. Margaret wanted it to be kept secret. And now Margaret was dead, and the notebook might be the only way to find out why.

Faye pulled the drawer open and took out the notebook.

Time to look again. More carefully this time.

———

SHE OPENED her grandmother's notebook—Margaret's last

gift to her—and began a systematic study. Tiny settled at her feet, a steady warmth that eased her nerves.

Margaret's handwriting in the margins was meticulous, each entry dated and organized. Property transfers. Shell company names. Initials scattered throughout like a code waiting to be cracked.

Faye had focused on the Harper Family Trust entry before —Lot 47, the lighthouse keeper's cottage. But now she forced herself to look at the bigger picture. What pattern was Margaret seeing in Bee's notebook.

She grabbed a notepad and began making her own list.

Coastal Heritage Holdings—appeared twelve times, always as the buyer. Yves had mentioned this name. His cousin's boat repair shop.

Butternut Bay Development LLC—appeared eight times, mostly waterfront properties.

Heritage Restoration Partners—appeared five times, connected to historic buildings.

Three different company names, but Margaret had drawn lines connecting them, with a single word written in the margin: *SAME?*

Faye turned more pages. The initials appeared again—but Margaret's hasty shorthand made them difficult to decipher. P.G.? P.C.? R.G.? The cramped handwriting could have been any of them. C.S. was clearer, and O.W., H.L. Some circled, some crossed out, some with question marks beside them. Near the back, Margaret had created a chart—dates in one column, initials in another, property descriptions in a third.

And then Faye saw something that made her breath catch.

A page she'd missed before, tucked between two others. A list of names—not initials this time, but full names—with notes beside each one.

Peter Grayson—antiques appraisal, archive access, Rosewell connection? Debts? CHECK FURTHER

Charlotte Whitford—board influence, property committee, Janet Ellis letter (CRITICAL)—what is she hiding?

Chance Whitford—money manager, offshore accounts? Follow the signatures

Noel—deliveries, doesn't ask questions, paid in cash

Faye stared at the page. Margaret had been building a case. Not just tracking property transfers, but identifying the people involved. The players in whatever scheme was reshaping Butternut Cove. But the notes were frustratingly incomplete—questions rather than answers, suspicions rather than proof. Any of them could be the killer. Charlotte, with her cold eyes and her threats to Margaret. Peter, with his archive access and his mysterious debts. Even Arthur himself couldn't be entirely ruled out—he'd had the most opportunity, and Margaret's notes mentioned "Whitford property disputes, 1987—LOOK DEEPER."

Three primary suspects. Peter Grayson, with his archive access and possible Rand connection. Charlotte Whitford, desperate to protect some secret involving her mother. And Kent Blake, whose chemistry expertise and long grudge against Arthur suddenly seemed more sinister.

She thought of Peter at the Ball, smooth and probing. *Any progress? I imagine you must be eager to clear your name.* The way his eyes had flickered when she said *the truth always comes out.* But was that guilt—or simply the calculation of a man protecting his business interests?

But then she thought of Charlotte at the Ball, her cold eyes meeting Faye's across the room. *Some things are better left buried.* And Kent, with his chemistry knowledge, his old grudge against Arthur, his convenient access to the archives as a "preservation consultant." Either of them could have poisoned those cookies just as easily as Peter.

Noel had made deliveries for half the town that day—including Peter, Kent, and several trips to Beacon Hall for the Historical Society. Paid in cash. Doesn't ask questions. But that didn't make him complicit—it just meant anyone could have used him as an unwitting courier.

The pieces were starting to fit together. Not a complete picture yet, but the outline of one.

The doorbell rang.

———

FAYE SWEPT the notebook and her notes into a pile and shoved them back in the drawer just as Tiny's bark announced the visitor. She smoothed her hair, took a breath, and opened the door.

Luke Grayson stood on her porch, looking like he hadn't slept. His coat was rumpled, his tie loosened, and there were shadows under his eyes that spoke of a long night.

"Detective." She stepped back to let him in. "Coffee?"

"God, yes."

She led him to the kitchen, poured him a cup, and watched him drink half of it in one long swallow. Tiny had positioned himself between them, not threatening, but watchful.

"Long night?" Faye asked.

"You could say that." Luke set down the cup and rubbed his face. "I've been at the station since we left the Ball. Kent Blake's statement, forensics reports, interviews with everyone who was near the serving area." He shook his head. "Someone tried to kill Arthur Whitford in front of three hundred people, and no one saw anything useful."

"The person who gave Allison the plate—"

"Wore gloves and disappeared into the crowd." Luke's frustration was palpable. "Professional. Careful. This wasn't someone's first time."

Faye thought of Margaret, poisoned in the archives. The same method. The same careful planning.

"What about the poison itself?"

"Preliminary results suggest cyanide—same as the cookies that killed Margaret. The almond scent is a giveaway."

Faye was quick to respond. "Exactly as I said."

Luke met her eyes. "We're dealing with the same killer, Faye. Someone who knows what they're doing and isn't afraid to do it again."

"And Kent?"

"Released this morning. His prints were on the knife, but it was clearly used for his idiotic prank, not the poisoning. The poisoned pudding came from a different source entirely— someone tampered with a slice in the kitchen before Allison picked it up." Luke sighed. "Kent Blake is guilty of being a petty, jealous fool, but he's not our killer."

"There's something else," Luke said, almost as an afterthought. "Kent mentioned something interesting during his interview. Said he'd noticed Peter Grayson selling family heirlooms through his shop lately. Silver, antique jewelry, pieces Kent recognized from the Grayson estate." He shrugged. "Kent was mostly complaining that Peter under-priced them—said a man doesn't sell his grandmother's silver unless he's desperate."

Desperate. The word echoed in Faye's mind. Peter's phone call at the Ball. The SALE signs at his shop she'd noticed. Now this.

"I could have told you that."

Luke's eyebrows rose. "You saw him tamper with the pudding?"

"During Dean's performance. He cut a slice and hid it in his pocket, then stashed the knife under the tablecloth." Faye shrugged. "I was going to tell you, but then everything happened so fast."

"And you didn't think that was relevant information?"

"I thought it was a prank. Which it was." She met his gaze steadily. "I wasn't trying to hide anything, Luke and it was all uncovered so quickly that I not need to say anything. I just had bigger things on my mind. Like someone trying to murder Arthur."

Luke held her gaze for a long moment, then nodded slowly. "Fair enough." He finished his coffee and set the cup down. "There's something else. The reason I came by."

"Yes?"

"Your café. The crime scene tape comes down this morning. Health department cleared the kitchen late yesterday. Then reopen whenever you're ready."

Relief flooded through her—real, physical relief that made her knees weak. "I'll reopen tomorrow."

"Monday morning. Merry Christmas." Luke's smile was tired but genuine. "I know it's been hard, Faye. Having your livelihood shut down, your name dragged through the gossip mill. This doesn't make up for any of that, but at least you can start to rebuild."

"Thank you." The words felt inadequate. "Luke, I... thank you."

He stood to leave, then paused at the kitchen door. "One more thing. The note Margaret left in your cookbook—we recovered it this morning when we cleared the scene. I can't tell you what it says yet, but..." He hesitated. "It confirms what we suspected. Margaret knew something dangerous. Something people were willing to kill to keep quiet."

"Property transfers," Faye said quietly. "Shell companies buying up the town."

Luke's eyes sharpened. "How do you know that?"

Faye's heart hammered. She could tell him about the notebook now. She should tell him. But the words that came out were different.

"Margaret mentioned it when she came to see me. Before... before she died. She was scared, Luke. She said people were buying up Butternut Cove piece by piece, and no one was paying attention."

It wasn't a lie. Not exactly. But it wasn't the whole truth

either, and Faye felt the weight of that omission settle on her conscience.

Luke studied her for a moment—the Detective's gaze, assessing, probing. Then he nodded.

"If you think of anything else—anything at all—you'll tell me?"

"Of course."

He left, and Faye stood in her kitchen, the notebook hidden in the drawer behind her, and wondered what kind of person she was becoming.

Luke had believed her. That was the worst part. He'd looked at her with those steady eyes, and he'd trusted her, and she'd lied to his face.

I'm fine, she'd said a thousand times when she wasn't. But this was different. This wasn't performing for people who didn't really want to know the truth. This was betraying someone who actually cared.

Tiny whined softly, pressing his nose against Faye's hand. Even the dog knew something was wrong.

"I know, good boy," Faye whispered. "I don't like it either."

———

BY AFTERNOON, the news had spread through Butternut Cove like wildfire.

Faye walked Tiny through town, partly for exercise and partly to gauge the temperature. The whispers had changed. Before the Ball, they'd been about her—the outsider, the suspect, the woman whose bakery box had been found beside a body. Now they were about Arthur, about the poisoning, about the killer who walked among them.

"Did you hear? Someone tried to poison Arthur Whitford right there at the Ball..."

"...those animals, can you imagine? Two dogs and a cat and a *goose* saved his life..."

"...Kent Blake arrested, but they let him go. Just a prank, they said..."

"...not safe in our own town anymore..."

Faye passed The Heirloom Table Café—still dark, but the yellow crime scene tape was gone from the door. Tomorrow, she could go back. Tomorrow, she could start rebuilding.

But first, she had questions that needed answers.

She found herself walking toward the harbor, toward the Lobsta Shack, toward Yves Brown and the information he might have.

⬚

THE LOBSTA SHACK was quiet on a Sunday afternoon, only a few regulars nursing beers and watching a football game on the ancient television behind the bar. Yves looked up when Faye entered with Tiny wearing his service dog jacket.

His weathered seaman's face creasing into something like welcome.

"Heard about last night," he said, pouring her coffee without being asked. "Heard your dog's a hero."

"He had help." Faye slid onto a stool, Tiny settling at her feet. "Yves, can I ask you something?"

"Ask."

"Peter Grayson. What do you know about him?"

Yves expression changed—a quick tightening around the eyes that told Faye she'd hit a nerve.

"Peter Grayson," he repeated slowly. "Antiques dealer. Old family, used to be money. His father ran the business into the ground—bad investments, gambling debts. By the time Peter inherited, there was nothing left but the name and a building full of dusty furniture."

"How did he survive? The business, I mean."

"That's the question, isn't it?" Yves leaned closer, his voice dropping. "About five years ago, Peter was done. Finished.

Couldn't make rent, couldn't pay suppliers. Everyone expected him to close up shop and crawl away."

"But he didn't did he, Faye observed."

"No. Suddenly, he had money again. New inventory, renovated showroom, suits that cost more than my truck." Yves shook his head. "Nobody knew where it came from. But there were rumors."

"What kind of rumors?"

"Rosewell." The name came out like something bitter. "Old money. The real kind. They've got a compound out on Rose Point—been there for generations. Nobody sees them much, but they own half the county. Word was, they bailed Peter out. Bought his debts, set him up again."

"Why would they do that?"

"Because now they own him and he does what they say." Yves's eyes were hard. "That's how it works with people like Rosewell. They don't give gifts. They make investments. And Peter Grayson—with his historical society connections, his access to records, his appraisal work that lets him into every old building in town—he's a useful man to own."

Faye thought of Margaret's notes: *Family debt—leverage.* It fit. It all fit.

"The property sales," she said slowly. "Coastal Heritage Holdings, Butternut Bay Development—those are Rosewell fronts, aren't they?"

Yves was quiet for a long moment. "I can't prove anything. Nobody can. That's how they set it up." He met her eyes. "But if someone were looking for answers—if someone wanted to know who was really pulling the strings—I'd tell them to follow the money. And I'd also tell them to be very, very careful."

"Margaret followed the money."

"And look what happened to her." Yves's voice was gentle but firm. "You've got good instincts, Faye. Good friends, good animals. But this thing—whatever Margaret stumbled onto—

it's bigger than one person. Bigger than one town, maybe. Don't let it swallow you too."

She thanked him and left money on the counter. Outside, the December late afternoon was fading toward evening, the sky heavy with clouds that promised more snow. Tiny pressed against her leg, warm and solid and reassuring.

Peter Grayson. Rosewell. A web of shell companies and property transfers and debts that could never be repaid.

Margaret had seen it all. And someone had killed her for it.

THAT EVENING, Faye sat at her kitchen table with Margaret's notebook open before her and a decision to make.

She'd been carrying this secret for days now. Hiding evidence. Lying—by omission, at least—to Luke. Telling herself it was what Margaret would have wanted, that she was honoring a dead woman's trust by keeping a secret.

But was she? Or was she just afraid? Afraid of what the notebook might reveal about her own family. Afraid of becoming more entangled in a conspiracy that had already killed one person and nearly killed another.

Tiny lay at her feet, watching with those wise, patient eyes. Ebenezer had settled for the night, his soft honks fading into sleep. The house was quiet, peaceful, a sanctuary against the darkness outside.

Faye looked at the notebook—at Margaret's careful handwriting, at the web of connections she'd painstakingly assembled.

She thought about Arthur, trembling in that sitting room, afraid to speak the truth even after someone had tried to kill him.

She thought about Charlotte's cold eyes, Oliver's silent presence, Peter's calculating smile.

She thought about Rosewell—faceless, powerful, pulling strings from their compound on the point.

A year ago—six months ago—she would have let it go. Would have told herself it wasn't her problem, wasn't her fight. She was just a café owner. Just a widow trying to rebuild her life. She didn't have the strength for other people's battles.

But Margaret had been just an archivist. Just a woman who loved history and couldn't look away from an uncomfortable truth.

And now Margaret was dead.

Faye closed the notebook and made a decision. Tomorrow, she would stop hiding. Tomorrow, she would tell Luke everything.

Tomorrow, she would reopen the café. She would smile and serve coffee and pretend everything was normal. But she would also watch. Listen. Gather what information she could.

And when she had enough—when she understood the full picture of what Margaret had discovered—she would go to Luke. She would tell him everything. Hand over the notebook and let the official investigation take its course.

She closed the notebook and put it back in the drawer. Then she turned off the lights, called Tiny to her side, and went to bed.

Tomorrow, *The Heirloom Table Café* would reopen.

Tomorrow, the real sorting through what she knew would begin.

12

Back to Business

MONDAY, DECEMBER 22ND.
THREE DAYS UNTIL CHRISTMAS.

Faye stood outside *The Heirloom Table Café* at six in the morning, keys in hand, breath misting in the cold December air. The yellow crime scene tape was gone. The windows were dark. The Christmas wreath she'd hung—was it really just a week ago? —still adorned the door, its dried oranges and cinnamon stick a stubborn reminder that the season of joy continued whether anyone felt joyful or not.

Tiny pressed against her leg, patient and steady.

"Here we go, honey," Faye murmured, and turned the key in the lock.

The café smelled stale—closed air, cold ovens, the faint chemical residue of whatever the forensics team had used. Faye stood in the doorway, letting her eyes adjust to the darkness, and felt something loosen in her chest. This was still hers. Despite everything, this was still hers.

She flipped on the lights and got to work.

———

BY SEVEN-THIRTY, the café was transformed. Windows thrown open to air out the staleness, counters and tables wiped down, ovens warming, the espresso machine hissing and gurgling like an old friend waking from sleep. Faye had made a quick batch of scones—nothing fancy, just something to fill the display case—and the smell of butter and sugar began to chase away the shadows.

Tessa arrived at eight, bearing a box of supplies from the general store and a fierce hug that nearly knocked Faye off her feet.

"You're really doing this," Tessa said, looking around at the café with something like wonder. "I wasn't sure you would."

"Neither was I." Faye wiped her hands on her apron. "But this is my home, Tessa. My livelihood. I'm not going to let fear chase me away."

"That's my girl." Tessa squeezed her arm. "Now put me to work. What do you need?"

They worked side by side through the morning prep, falling into the familiar rhythm of café life.

Tiny settled into his usual spot near the counter, well out of the way, greeting early customers with dignified wags of his tail.

The first visitor was Mr. Plum, one of her regulars, who ordered his usual black coffee and blueberry muffin as if nothing had happened.

"Glad you're back," he said gruffly, leaving exact change on the counter. "Place wasn't the same without you."

After that, the trickle became a stream. Some customers

came out of genuine support, offering warm words and larger-than-usual tips. Others came out of curiosity—Faye could see it in their eyes, the way they glanced around the café as if expecting to find bloodstains or police tape. A few came with barely concealed hostility, ordering their drinks with clipped words and leaving without a thank you.

Faye served them all with the same steady smile, the same careful attention to their orders. This was her job. This was who she was. She wouldn't give anyone the satisfaction of seeing her break.

———

THE LUNCH RUSH had just ended when Noel pushed through the door, his delivery bag slung over one shoulder. He looked tired—dark circles under his eyes, shoulders hunched against the cold—and when he saw Faye, something flickered across his face. Guilt? Fear? She couldn't quite read it.

"Faye." He approached the counter hesitantly. "I heard you were open again. Wanted to... I mean, I thought I should..."

"Sit down, Noel." Faye gestured to a stool. "Let me get you something. Coffee? A grilled cheese?"

He sat, his bag dropping to the floor with a heavy thump. "Coffee would be good. Thanks."

She poured him a cup and slid it across to him, then leaned against the counter waiting. Noel wrapped his hands around the mug but didn't drink, staring into the dark liquid as if it held answers.

"I've been thinking," he said finally. "About that day. The day Miss Ellis died."

Faye's heart rate quickened, but she kept her voice calm. "What about it?"

"The deliveries I made. The packages." Noel looked up, and she saw real distress in his eyes. "The police asked me about them. Asked who gave me what, where I took it. I told them everything I could remember, but..."

"But?"

"There was one package. Mr. Grayson gave it to me on the street—you saw, I think. Brown paper, about this big." He held his hands apart, indicating a rectangular shape. "He paid me twenty dollars to take it to Beacon Hall. Said it was a donation for the archives. Historical documents or something."

"Did you deliver it?" she asked carefully.

"I left it at the back entrance, like he said. There's a drop box there for after-hours donations." Noel's voice cracked. "But Faye, I've been thinking. What if it wasn't documents? What if it was..." He couldn't finish.

"Did you tell the police this?"

"I told them about all my deliveries. But I didn't think—I didn't realize—"He put his head in his hands. "Mr. Grayson's always been nice to me. Gives me work when I need it. Pays fair. I never thought he could be involved in something like this."

Faye came around the counter and put a hand on his shoulder. "Noel, listen to me. You didn't do anything wrong. You made a delivery—that's your job. Whatever was in that package, whatever happened afterward, that's not on you."

The words came out anguished. "What if I carried the poison that killed her?"

"You didn't know. You couldn't have known." Faye squeezed his shoulder. "The important thing now is that you're going to talk with Detective Grayson. Let them figure out the rest."

Noel nodded slowly, some of the tension easing from his shoulders. He drank his coffee in silence, and when he left, he pressed a crumpled five-dollar bill into her hand despite her protests.

"For the coffee," he said. "And for listening."

After he left, Faye stood at the window, watching him disappear down the street.

Poor Noel. He meant no harm—just did his deliveries and trusted the world to be fair. The town looked after him because someone should.

But Peter Grayson.

A package delivered to Beacon Hall the same day Margaret died.

Another piece of the puzzle clicked quietly into place.

———

HE CAME in at three o'clock, just as the afternoon lull settled over the café.

Peter Grayson pushed through the door with the casual confidence of a man who belonged everywhere, his cashmere coat perfectly tailored, his silver hair swept back from his forehead. He surveyed the café with a practiced eye—the kind of look Faye had seen him use when appraising antiques—before settling on her with a smile.

"Faye. How delightful to see you back in business."

Faye kept her expression pleasant. "Peter Grayson. What can I get you?"

"Just coffee. Black." He settled onto a stool, crossing his legs with elegant precision. "I was so pleased to hear you'd reopened. After everything that's happened, lesser women might have given up."

"I'm not easily discouraged." She poured his coffee, set it before him. "Cream and sugar are on the counter if you change your mind."

"I never do." Peter lifted the cup, inhaled the steam. "Excellent brew. You have a gift, Faye."

"Thank you."

They regarded each other across the counter—two people

who both knew more than they were saying, each trying to read the other without revealing themselves.

"Terrible business at the Ball," Peter said conversationally. "Poor Arthur. To think someone would try such a thing, right there in front of everyone." He shook his head. "The world has become a dangerous place."

"It certainly has."

"I understand your dog was quite the hero. And Callie Sweet's remarkable cat." Peter's smile widened. "Animals have such keen instincts, don't they? They sense things we miss."

Was that a threat? A warning? Faye couldn't tell, and she didn't like not being able to tell.

"They do," she agreed. "Tiny's saved my life more than once. He often knows when something's wrong before I do."

At the mention of his name, Tiny lifted his head from his bed by the counter. Her dark eyes fixed on Peter, and a low sound rumbled in his chest—not quite a growl, but something close to it.

Peter's smile flickered. Just for a moment, but Faye saw it.

"Well." He set down his cup, reaching for his wallet. "I won't keep you. I'm sure you have much to do, getting back on your feet." He laid a ten-dollar bill on the counter—far more than the coffee was worth. "Keep the change. Consider it a welcome-back gift."

"That's very generous."

"I believe in supporting local businesses." Peter rose, buttoning his coat. "Butternut Cove is such a special place. We must all do our part to preserve it."

He moved toward the door, then paused, looking back over his shoulder.

"Oh, one more thing. I understand the police recovered some materials from Margaret Ellis's effects. Notes, documents, that sort of thing." His eyes were sharp despite his casual tone. "I don't suppose she left anything with you?

Before she died, I mean. She was always so meticulous about her research."

Faye's heart stopped. Just for a beat, but long enough that she had to fight to keep her expression neutral.

"Margaret came in for coffee sometimes," she said carefully. "We talked about the archives, the Historical Society. But she never gave me anything."

It was a lie. A direct, deliberate lie. And from the way Peter studied her face, she wasn't sure he believed it.

"Hmm." He held her gaze for a long moment. "Well. If anything does turn up, I'm sure you'll do the right thing and notify the authorities." His smile was thin. "Good day, Faye."

The door closed behind him, and Faye let out a breath of repressed anxiety.

Maybe he knew. Or at least, he suspected. Why else would he ask about Margaret's research? Why else would he come here, today of all days, to probe and test and watch her reactions?

Tiny had risen from his wicker chair near the front windows, sensing Faye's distress, and pressed against her leg. Her body was tense, her eyes still fixed on the door where Peter had disappeared.

"I know, honey," Faye murmured. "I don't trust him either."

Her hands were shaking. She noticed it distantly, the way she might notice a stranger trembling across a room. When had she started shaking?

I'm scared, she admitted to herself. Not I'm fine. Not I can handle this. Just the truth, plain and unvarnished.

Somehow, admitting it made it easier to breathe.

———

ROSE FAIRWEATHER ARRIVED at closing time, just as Faye was wiping down the last tables.

She looked exhausted—dark circles under her eyes, her usually immaculate appearance slightly disheveled. Her designer coat was buttoned wrong, and her hair had escaped its careful arrangement to hang in wisps around her face.

"Faye." Rose glanced around the empty café. "Could we talk? Privately?"

Faye locked the door and flipped the sign to CLOSED. "Of course. Sit down. Can I get you anything?"

"Tea, if you have it. Something calming." Rose sank into a chair as if her legs couldn't hold her anymore. "Chamomile, maybe."

Faye made the tea, brought it to the table, and sat across from Rose. Tiny positioned himself nearby, watchful but not threatening.

Tessa is the back helping me clean up. She can't hear what we say.

"I've made a terrible mistake," Rose said without preamble. "I should have spoken up sooner. I should have told someone. But I was scared, and I thought—" She pressed a hand to her throat, composing herself. "I thought if I stayed quiet, it would all go away."

"What are you talking about, Rose?"

"The archives. What Margaret found." Rose's hands trembled around her teacup. "I knew. Not everything, but... I knew she'd discovered something. Something about the property transfers. Something about the people involved."

Faye kept her voice steady. And asked gently. "What did you know?"

"I overheard a conversation. A few weeks ago, in the archives. Charlotte Whitford came to see Margaret—which was odd, because Charlotte never comes to the archives. She sends one of her assistants." Rose took a sip of tea, steadying herself. "They didn't know I was there. I was in the back room, organizing some files that had just come in."

"What did they talk about?"

"Charlotte was... threatening her. In that polite, cold way she has. Saying that Margaret needed to be more careful with her research. That some things were better left buried. That there were people who wouldn't appreciate having old secrets dug up."

"What secrets?"

"I don't know the details. But Charlotte mentioned something about her family—about her mother, I think. Janet. And she mentioned..." Rose hesitated. "She mentioned a child. A daughter. Someone Charlotte had gone to great lengths to keep hidden."

Faye remembered Margaret's notes: *Charlotte Whitford—something to hide? See Janet Ellis letter.* Janet Ellis. Margaret's grandmother? Her mother? Someone who knew Charlotte's secret.

"Charlotte has a secret child?" Faye queried thoughtfully.

"Had. Has. I don't know." Rose shook her head. "She said something about how Margaret's grandmother had promised to keep it quiet. That Janet Ellis had been a trusted friend, and Margaret was betraying that trust by digging through old records."

"And Margaret? What did she say?"

"She said the truth mattered. That people deserved to know what had been done to this town, even if it meant uncomfortable revelations." Rose's voice broke. "She was so brave. And I just... I hid, frozen in the back room under the desk and didn't say anything. Not to Margaret, not to anyone. And now she's dead."

"You couldn't have known what would happen."

"Couldn't I?" Rose looked up, her eyes red-rimmed. "Charlotte was threatening her. I heard it. And I did nothing." She set down her teacup. "I'm telling you now because I can't hold it in anymore. And because..."

"Because?"

"Because I think you're the only person in this town who

cares about the truth as much as Margaret did." Rose stood, gathering her coat. "I'm going to the police now. Talking to you has helped give me the courage to tell Detective Grayson everything I told you. But I wanted you to know first. In case..." She didn't finish the sentence.

"In case something happens to you," Faye finished quietly.

Rose nodded, her face pale. "Be careful, Faye. These people—Charlotte whoever else is involved—they've already killed once. They tried again at the Ball. They won't stop until they're sure their secrets are safe."

She left, and Faye sat alone at the counter in her closed café, the pieces of the puzzle rearranging themselves in her mind.

The sounds of Tessa and the dishwasher in the background.

went home and Faye sat alone at her counter at the café.

The puzzle pieces turned in her mind. Charlotte, with her secret and her threats. Peter, with his debts and his archive access. Kent, with his chemistry expertise and his knowledge of Peter's desperation.

It could still be Kent. He had the knowledge to procure and administer poison—his preservation work gave him access to all sorts of dangerous compounds. And his grudge against Arthur ran deep, years of simmering resentment over a rejected application.

Or Charlotte, protecting a secret so devastating she'd threatened Margaret's life over it. Charlotte, who had the most to lose her hidden daughter ever came to light. If there even was a hidden daughter.

But the Rosewell connection kept pulling her back to Peter. The shell companies. The debt. The way Rosewell had bailed him out five years ago, turning him into their secret pawn.

If she was going to prove anything, she needed more. She needed to understand the full scope of what Margaret had discovered. And she needed to do it before the killer realized how close she was getting.

Charlotte's secret child? Peter's package to the archives? Rosewell, pulling strings from behind the scenes? Shell companies and property transfers and debts that could never be repaid?

Margaret had seen the whole picture. She'd understood how it all connected.

And someone had killed her for it. But Faye was still in the dark about how it all came together.

⊏⊐

THAT NIGHT, Faye sat at her kitchen table with Margaret's notebook, her own notepad, and a growing sense of dread.

She had been approaching this all wrong.

She'd been searching for a single killer, a single motive, a single thread that could neatly explain everything. But this wasn't a simple murder. It was a conspiracy—multiple people, multiple motives, all tied together by money, secrets, and the systematic dismantling of Butternut Cove.

She picked up her pen and began to write.

Viable suspects

Rose Fairweather—present at Margaret's death.

Noel—the town's delivery boy.

Henry Lawson—Arthur Whitford's devoted assistant.

Rosewell—the money behind it all. Buying up the town through shell companies. Using Peter Grayson as their agent because they owned his debts.

Peter Grayson—the hands. Access to the archives. Appraisal work. Connections throughout town. Had a package delivered to Beacon Hall the day Margaret died.

Charlotte Whitford—the fear. A secret Margaret uncovered. Threatened Margaret weeks before her death. Would do anything to protect her reputation and her fortune.

Chance Whitford—the enabler. Charlotte's brother. Manager of the family trust. Signs the documents. Stays silent and lets it all happen.

Kent Blake—should be on this list. Chemistry expert. Preservation specialist. Envious of Gerald. Resentful.

Arthur Whitford—the latest target. Knew too much. Planned to expose everything at the Ball. Someone tried to silence him before he could speak.

She turned the page and drew another line.

Cleared suspects. Or something more complicated than that.

Rose Fairweather—an associate archivist at Beacon Hall. Present at Margaret's death, but no longer a suspect. A witness now. Afraid. Sitting on information that could put her in danger—or protect her.

Noel—Kind. Earnest. Easily pressured, easily used. The perfect pawn for someone else's plan, but not a murderer.

Henry Lawson—Deeply affected by Margaret's death. His grief felt genuine, unguarded. More collateral damage than culprit.

Arthur Whitford—no longer a suspect, but still not safe. Knows too much. Holds proof too dangerous to keep. A target, whether he realizes it or not.

Faye set her pen aside, rubbing her temples.

Being cleared didn't mean being safe.

Faye stared at the list.

Something was still missing.

The connection.

- The person who hadn't just benefited from the plan—but had carried it out.
- The one who poisoned Margaret.
- The one who poisoned the slice of figgy pudding.
- The one who had used *her* café to do it.
- Someone with access.

- Opportunity.
- And the cold-blooded resolve to kill.
- And why me?
- Peter had access.
- Peter had motive—his debts, his obligations to the Rosewells.

But was Peter capable of murder?

She thought of Peter's smooth smile, his probing questions, the way he'd asked—too casually—about Margaret's research. She remembered the calculation in his eyes when she'd said the truth always comes out.

Yes. She believed he was capable.

But belief wasn't proof. Not yet. She needed something solid—something that placed Peter not just near the conspiracy, but at the heart of it.

She glanced back at the other names.

Rosewell. Charlotte. Chance. Kent.

Pieces on the board. All with secrets. All with something to lose.

But only one of them had lied to her more than once.

Faye leaned back in her chair.

The net was tightening.

Tiny rested his head against her knee, and she stroked the soft velvet of his ears, drawing comfort from the steady warmth of him.

"We're close, honey," she murmured. "I can feel it."

Tiny's tail thumped once against the floor.

Faye closed her notebook and slid it back beside Margaret's. She checked the locks on the doors, turned out the lights, and went to bed with Tiny stretched at her feet.

Two days until Christmas.

Two days to find a killer.

She wasn't fine. She might never be fine again.

But she was done pretending.

13

The Truth Emerges
TUESDAY, DECEMBER 23RD.
TWO DAYS UNTIL CHRISTMAS.

The call from Luke came at seven in the morning, before Faye had even finished her first cup of coffee while Tessa continued creating Christmas decorations.

"Rose Fairweather gave her statement," he said without preamble. "About Charlotte Whitford threatening Margaret. About the secret Charlotte was trying to protect."

Faye set down her mug. "And?"

"And it corroborates what we found in Margaret's note— the one she hid in your cookbook." Luke's voice was tight with controlled excitement. "Margaret wrote that Charlotte Whitford had a child out of wedlock in 1985. A daughter. The pregnancy was concealed, the child given up for adoption.

Charlotte's mother, Helen and Janet Ellis helped arrange the whole thing."

"Janet Ellis. Margaret's mother?" Faye asked.

"Exactly. Which is how Margaret found out. She was going through her mother's papers after Janet died last year and discovered letters, documents, the whole story." Luke paused. "But here's the thing, Faye. Charlotte's secret is damaging, sure. Embarrassing. But it's not enough to kill over. Not in 2025. Society's changed. People wouldn't care as much as Charlotte fears."

"Unless there's more to it." Faye suggests.

"Unless there's more to it," Luke agreed. "And I think there is. The property transfers Margaret was tracking—they all connect back to the same period. The same shell companies. The same people." He took a breath. "I need you to come to the station, Faye. There's something I want to show you."

Faye looked at Tiny, who had lifted his head at the tension in the room. "I'll can be there in an hour." Faye hung up the phone.

━━

THE POLICE STATION WAS QUIET, most of the staff occupied with last-minute Christmas preparations rather than active cases. Luke led Faye to a small conference room where files and photographs covered the table in organized chaos.

"Close the door," he said.

She did, and Tiny settled at her feet, a solid, steady presence.

"What I'm about to show you doesn't leave this room." Luke's expression was serious. "Officially, you're still a person of interest in this case. But off the record—" He shook his head. "Off the record, I know you didn't do this. And I think you know more than you've told me."

Faye's heart hammered. The notebook. He was talking about the notebook.

"Luke—"

"Don't." He held up a hand. "I'm not asking you to incriminate yourself. I'm asking you to help me catch a killer." He gestured to the table. "Look at this."

Faye moved closer. The photographs showed evidence bags—a cookie box, packaging materials, a small vial. The files contained forensic reports, witness statements, property records.

"The cookie that killed Margaret was laced with cyanide," Luke said. "Same compound used in the pudding at the Ball. Our lab traced the source to a specialty chemical supplier in Boston—the kind that sells to antique restorers for treating furniture."

"Antique restorers. Peter Grayson." Faye thinks to herself.

"We pulled purchase records," Luke continued. "Peter Grayson bought a quantity of potassium cyanide six months ago. Claimed it was for restoring a Victorian writing desk with insect damage."

"That's not enough for an arrest," Faye said slowly. "Lots of restorers use cyanide."

"No. But this might be." Luke slid a photograph across the table. "We found a partial fingerprint on the inside of one of your bakery box—the one left beside Margaret's body. It doesn't match you, doesn't match Margaret, doesn't match anyone on your staff."

Faye stared at the photograph—a close-up of a smudged print, barely visible against the white cardboard.

"We ran it through the system," Luke said. "No match in any criminal database. But we can compel a comparison if we have a suspect. And with Noel's statement about the package Peter gave him—"

"You have enough for a warrant." Faye said.

"We have enough to ask questions. Officially." Luke leaned

back in his chair. "The Chief is nervous. Peter Grayson has connections—the Historical Society, old families, people who donate to political campaigns. But the evidence is building. If that fingerprint matches Peter's..."

"Then you have him." Faye remarked.

"Then we have him." Luke met her eyes. "But here's the problem. Peter knows we're closing in. He came to see you yesterday—yes, I know about that, Tessa told me—and he asked about Margaret's research. He's getting nervous. Nervous people do desperate things."

"You think he might run?"

"I think he might do something worse." Luke's voice was grim. "Which is why I need to know, Faye—is there anything else? Anything you haven't told me that could help nail this down?"

The notebook burned in her conscience. Margaret's careful handwriting, her web of connections, her notes about Peter and the Rosewell and Charlotte's secret.

She could lie. She'd done it before—to Luke, to herself, to everyone who asked how she was doing. *I'm fine.* The words were so easy, so practiced. They kept people at a safe distance. They kept her heart protected.

But Margaret had trusted her with the truth. And Margaret was dead because someone else had chosen lies over honesty, self-protection over courage.

Faye was tired of hiding. Tired of walls. Tired of being *fine* when she wasn't.

"Yes," Faye said quietly. "There is."

⸺

SHE TOLD HIM EVERYTHING.

About Margaret pressing the notebook into her hands. About hiding it, studying it, wrestling with whether to turn it over. About the names and dates and shell companies, about

Peter's debts and the Rosewell influence, about the page that listed everyone involved and their roles in the scheme.

Luke listened without interrupting, his face unreadable. When she finished, he was quiet for a long moment.

"You've been sitting on this for days," he said finally. "Evidence in a murder investigation."

"I know." Faye couldn't meet his eyes. "I was scared. Confused. Margaret told me not to tell anyone, and then she was dead, and I didn't know who to trust."

"You could have trusted me."

"Could I?" She looked up. "Luke, this conspiracy reaches into the highest levels of Butternut Cove society. Charlotte Whitford. The Rosewell. People with money and influence and the power to make problems disappear. How was I supposed to know you weren't part of it?"

"Because I'm trying to solve Margaret's murder, not cover it up." His voice was sharp, but beneath the anger, she heard hurt. "I thought we were on the same side."

"We are. We always were." Faye reached across the table, not quite touching his hand. "I'm sorry, Luke. I made the wrong call. But I'm telling you now. Everything."

The words hung in the air between them—*everything*—and Faye realized she meant it. Not just the notebook. Not just the evidence. She was offering him her trust, fragile and hard-won, knowing he could break it.

It was terrifying. It was also, strangely, a relief.

He studied her face for a long moment, then nodded slowly.

"The notebook. Where is it?"

"At my house. In the kitchen drawer."

"I need it. Right away. It's evidence."

Luke exhaled slowly, some of the tension leaving his shoulders. "This changes things. Margaret's notes, combined with the fingerprint evidence, Noel's statement, and Rose's testimony—we might actually be able to build a case."

"Against Peter?" Faye asked.

"Against all of them, eventually. But Peter first. He's the weak link—the one who actually committed the murder. If we can break him, he might give up the others."

Luke's phone buzzed sharply. He glanced at the screen and answered.

"That was dispatch," he said. "A patrol just spotted Peter Grayson's car near the cliffs."

Luke stayed where he was, phone still in hand. "Faye, I need to stay with this. Go home. Stay inside. I'll come by for the notebook within the hour."

Then, more quietly:

"Don't answer the door for anyone except me. Peter knows the net is closing. I don't know what he might do."

⊏⊐

THE CALL CAME as Faye was walking home, Tiny at her side.

"Faye?" Arthur Whitford's voice was strained. "I need to see you. Today. It's urgent."

"Arthur, I'm not sure that's a good idea. The police—"

"The police can't help me." There was real fear in his voice. "Charlotte and Oliver have gone to visit his family in Boston for the holiday and Beatrice, my sister joined them. I'm alone in this house, and I've received... I've received a threat. Someone knows I was going to expose them at the Ball. Someone knows I still have the documents Margaret gave me before she died."

Faye stopped walking. "Margaret gave you documents?"

"Yes, Originals and copies. Backup copies of everything she'd found. She didn't trust the archives—said someone had been going through her files." Arthur's breath was ragged. "I should have given them to the police immediately. But I was afraid. Charlotte, Chance—they're my family. I thought I could handle it quietly. I thought—"

"Arthur, listen to me. Call Luke Grayson right now. Tell him everything you just told me."

"I can't. Not yet. There are things—family things—that I need to explain first. Things that will make more sense if I show you the documents first." His voice dropped. "Please, Faye. You're the only person in this town I trust. Margaret trusted you. That's enough for me."

Faye hesitated. Luke had told her to go home, stay safe, wait for him. But Arthur had documents. Evidence. The proof she'd been looking for.

"Where are you?" Faye asked.

"At the house. The Whitford estate on Cliff Road. Do you know it?"

Everyone knew it. The grand Victorian mansion over-looking the ocean and the northern coast with Salem being the first visible town, one of the oldest and finest houses in Butternut Cove.

"I'll be there in twenty minutes," Faye said. "But Arthur— I'm calling Luke as soon as we're done. Whatever you show me, whatever you tell me, it goes to the police."

"Agreed." Relief flooded his voice. "Thank you, Faye. Thank you."

She hung up and looked down at Tiny, who was watching her with those wise, patient eyes.

"I know," Faye said. "It's probably a bad idea. But we're going anyway."

Tiny's tail wagged once. Not approval, exactly. More like: *If you're going, I'm going with you.*

"That's the deal," Faye agreed. *"Always."*

———

THE WHITFORD ESTATE loomed against the grey December sky, its Victorian turrets and gables giving it the look of a castle from a fairy tale—or a Gothic novel. The gardens were winter-bare, the fountain silent, the windows dark except for a single light in what Faye guessed was the study.

Arthur met her at the door, looking more fragile than she'd ever seen him. He'd lost weight since the Ball—just three days ago, but it felt like a lifetime—and his hands trembled as he ushered her inside.

"Thank you for coming." He glanced at Tiny, managed a weak smile. "And you brought your guardian. Good. I feel safer already."

Tiny whined softly, shifting his weight from paw to paw.

"He needs a comfort stop," Faye said apologetically. "The drive—"

"Of course." Arthur gestured toward the back of the house. "There's a dog door in the kitchen entrance—years ago I had wolfhounds. He can let himself into the walled garden and back."

Faye unclipped Tiny's leash and walked with him to the kitchen, nails clicking on the marble floor. "Go on, honey."

Faye watched Tiny disappear through the dog door, then turned back to Arthur.

"Come this way," Arthur said. "The documents are in the study."

―――

THE HOUSE WAS COLD, as if the heating had been turned down or off entirely. Their footsteps echoed on marble floors as Arthur led her through a grand foyer hung with oil paintings and into a wood-paneled study lined with books.

A fire burned in the grate—the only warmth in the house. Arthur gestured to a chair near the hearth and lowered himself into its twin, groaning slightly.

"The documents are in the safe," he said. "I'll show you everything. But first—there are things you need to understand. About my family. About Charlotte."

"Her secret child?" Faye asked.

Arthur nodded slowly. "You know about that. I wondered if Margaret had told you." He stared into the fire. "The child was born in 1985. Charlotte was twenty-three, unmarried, terrified of scandal. Her mother Janet—and Margaret's mother—helped arrange a private adoption. The child went to a good family. It was supposed to be the end of it."

"But it wasn't."

"No." Arthur's voice was heavy. "The child—a girl named Sylvie—found Charlotte two years ago. She wanted to know her birth mother. Wanted answers. Charlotte refused to meet her, refused to acknowledge her existence. Paid her off, actually. Gave her money to go away and stay away."

"That's so difficult." Faye said.

"Yes, for both of them." Arthur's sighed. "Charlotte cares more about appearances than people. Always has. But here's the thing—Margaret found out about Sylvie. Found the adoption records, the payoff, everything. And she was going to include it in her report about the property transfers."

"Why?" Faye asked. "What does Charlotte's secret child have to do with property?"

"Because Sylvie technically is an heir." Arthur met Faye's eyes. "The Whitford Family Trust—our family's entire fortune —passes to direct descendants. If it became known that Charlotte had a living child, that child would have a claim. A significant claim. Millions of dollars. Properties throughout the county. Including—" He paused. "Including the land that's been sold to those shell companies over the past five years."

Faye felt the pieces clicking into place. "The property transfers. They're not just about development. They're about hiding assets from a potential heir?"

"Exactly." Arthur rose, moving toward a painting on the wall. "Charlotte convinced Chance, her brother, to liquidate family holdings through shell companies—the Rosewell helped, took their cut—all to ensure that if Sylvie ever pressed her claim, there would be nothing left to claim."

Arthur paused, his hand moving to the side table beside his chair. His fingers found something underneath—a soft click.

"After what happened at the Ball, I had this installed," he said. "Silent alarm. Goes directly to the police station. Charlotte thought I was paranoid, but..." He shrugged. "After someone tries to poison you, a little paranoia seems warranted."

Faye filed the information away. Just in case.

He rose and moved toward a painting on the wall. He swung the painting aside, revealing a wall safe. "Margaret figured it all out. Traced every transaction. And she was going to expose it."

"Faye asked in amazement, so Charlotte had her killed."

"No." Arthur turned from the safe, documents in his hands. "Charlotte is many things, but she's not a murderer. She threatened Margaret, yes. Tried to buy her silence. But kill her?" He shook his head. "That was someone else. Someone with even more to lose."

"Peter Grayson?" Faye asked.

Arthur handed her the documents—originals in one stack and the other stack were the photocopies of deeds, bank transfers, correspondence. "Peter is the one who executed all the transactions. He's the one who knows where every dollar went, which properties were sold to whom, how the Rosewell profited. If Margaret's report had come out, Peter wouldn't just be exposed—he'd be prosecuted. Fraud, money laundering, conspiracy. He'd lose everything. Go to prison." Arthur's voice dropped. "He killed Margaret to protect himself. And he tried to kill me for the same reason."

Faye looked down at the documents in her hands. Names, dates, amounts. The paper trail that connected everything.

"This is it," she breathed. "This is the proof."

"Yes," Arthur said quietly. "I needed one person to understand why I didn't act sooner." Then sank back into his chair, exhausted.

"Take it. Give it to Detective Grayson. Let him do what I should have done from the beginning."

Faye asked in a tender tone "Why didn't you? Why keep this secret?"

"Because Charlotte is my niece. Because Chance is my nephew. Because exposing them means exposing my family." Arthur's eyes glistened. "But Margaret is dead. Someone tried to kill me. There's a line, Faye, and they crossed it. Family loyalty only goes so far."

Footsteps in the hallway. Slow. Deliberate. Coming closer.

Arthur's face went white.

14

Confrontation
TUESDAY, DECEMBER 23RD.

Peter Grayson stood in the doorway of Arthur's study, snow dusting the shoulders of his cashmere coat. He looked smaller than Faye remembered—not the composed, elegant antique dealer she'd known for years, but a man unraveling at the seams. His eyes darted to the documents spread across Arthur's desk, and something desperate flickered across his face.

"Peter." Arthur's voice was wary. "What are you doing here? Charlotte and Oliver are in Boston."

"I know." Peter stepped into the room, his gaze fixed on the papers. "I saw Faye's car in the drive. I thought—" He stopped, swallowed hard. "I need those documents, Arthur. The property records. Margaret's research."

Faye's heart beat faster, but she kept her voice steady. "Why would you need them, Peter?"

"Because they're mine." The desperation in his voice was unmistakable now. "Some of those records—the appraisals, the transfer documents—they have my signature. My hand-writing." He took another step toward the desk. "I can't let them become evidence."

Arthur moved to stand between Peter and the documents, his frail frame somehow resolute. "These papers aren't going anywhere, Peter. They're originals—the only copies that exist. Margaret was very particular about that. She said photocopies could be disputed, but originals tell the truth."

Something crumbled in Peter's expression. "Originals. Of course she kept originals." He laughed—a hollow, broken sound. "Margaret was always thorough."

"Thorough enough to figure out what you've been doing," Faye said quietly. "The shell companies. The inflated appraisals. That's why you killed her, isn't it? Because she traced it all back to you."

Peter flinched as if she'd struck him. "I didn't want to. You have to understand—I *liked* Margaret. Respected her. But she wouldn't stop digging." His voice cracked. "She was going to expose everything. The Rosewell, the property scheme, my role in all of it. I would have lost everything—the shop, my reputation, my freedom. I panicked."

"So you poisoned her." Faye's voice was calm, but her hands trembled at her sides. "With cookies from my café. You framed me."

"The boxes were everywhere. It was convenient." Peter's eyes were wet now, his composure completely gone. "I'm not a monster, Faye. I'm just a man who made terrible choices and couldn't find a way out."

"There's always a way out that doesn't involve murder."

Peter didn't answer. His gaze had drifted back to the docu-ments on Arthur's desk—specifically to a single sheet near the top. An appraisal form, Faye realized, with Peter's distinctive signature at the bottom.

"I just need that one page," he said, his voice dropping to something almost pleading. "Just that one. It's the only thing that directly ties me to—"

"No." Arthur's voice was firm. "These documents are evidence now. They belong to the police."

Peter's hand moved to his pocket, and Faye tensed—but what he withdrew wasn't a weapon. It was a lighter. Antique, silver, monogrammed. His fingers shook as he flicked it open.

"I'm sorry," he whispered. "I truly am."

He lunged for the desk.

Arthur was faster than Faye expected. The old man grabbed Peter's wrist, trying to wrestle the lighter away, but Peter was younger, stronger. The small flame danced between them as they struggled—and then Peter's shaking hand jerked sideways.

The flame kissed the edge of the heavy damask pillow on the leather chair.

For one horrible moment, Faye watched the fire catch—a tiny tongue of orange that bloomed with terrifying speed through the dry fabric—a sudden wash of heat licked across Faye's face.

Peter stumbled backward, his face white with shock. He hadn't meant to do that. She could see it in his eyes. He'd only wanted to destroy one piece of paper, and now—

Arthur moved.

The crystal pitcher on the side table—the one that had held water for his afternoon tea—was in his hands before Faye could react. He threw its contents at the chair in one decisive arc. Water splashed across the burning fabric, and the flames hissed and died, leaving nothing but a scorched streak and the acrid smell of singed cloth and leather.

What happened next would replay in Faye's memory for

years to come—a sequence of moments so swift and precise that they seemed choreographed by fate itself.

Tiny entered the room like a freight train—one hundred and forty pounds of Dane moving at full speed. He must have heard the commotion from the garden, found his way through the dog door, and tracked Faye's scent through the house. His ears were flat, his hackles raised, and he was making a sound Faye had never heard from him before—a deep, rumbling growl that seemed to vibrate through the floor.

Peter turned, lighter still clutched in his hand, and Tiny hit him square in the chest.

The impact wasn't vicious—Tiny was too well-trained for that—but it was unstoppable. Peter went down hard, the lighter skittering across the floor, and before he could move, Tiny was standing over him. Not biting. Not snarling. Just *there* —massive and immovable, one huge paw planted firmly on Peter's chest, dark eyes fixed on his face with an expression that said very clearly: *Don't.*

Peter didn't.

"Good boy," Faye breathed, her voice shaking. "Good, brave boy."

And then she heard it—sirens. Multiple vehicles, growing rapidly closer.

Arthur sagged against his desk, one hand pressed to his heart. "The silent alarm," he managed. "When I explained it to you," Arthur said, "I triggered it. Showing you the papers made me uneasy. It seemed… prudent."

The sirens grew louder. Tires crunched on gravel. Doors slammed.

She looked down at Peter Grayson, pinned beneath Tiny —this man who had killed Margaret, who had attempted to kill Arthur, who had framed her, who had just accidentally set fire to Arthur's study in a desperate attempt to save himself.

He looked pathetic now. Small. Frightened. He had admitted his guilt.

"It's over, Peter," she said quietly.

He closed his eyes. "I know."

———

LUKE GRAYSON APPEARED at the door with three officers behind him, his face tight with controlled urgency. He took in the scene—the scorched drapes, the scattered documents, Peter flat on his back with Tiny standing guard—and his shoulders dropped slightly with relief.

"Faye." He crossed to her in three quick strides. "Are you hurt?"

She opened her mouth to say *I'm fine*—the automatic response, the deflection she'd used for five years—and stopped. Caught herself.

"No," she said instead. "I'm shaking and my heart won't stop racing and I think I might cry." She managed a wobbly smile. "But we're alive. Arthur's alive. And Peter—" She gestured toward the pinned man. "He confessed. To poisoning Margaret. To the poisoning at the Ball. All of it."

Luke's eyes met hers, and she saw something warm there —respect, maybe, or something deeper. "We got two calls at once. Arthur's silent alarm, and Tessa—she said she had a bad feeling when you didn't come back. Then she came to the station. She's been pacing the station lobby for twenty minutes."

Of course. Tessa, who always knew when something was wrong.

Luke nodded to his officers. "Get him up. Read him his rights."

Faye touched Tiny's shoulder. "Release, boy. You can let go now."

Tiny stepped back, allowing the officers to haul Peter to his feet. The Dane nuzzled Faye's hand, his tail wagging slowly—not celebration, just relief. *We're okay. We did it.*

As they led Peter toward the door, he turned back. His face was gray, defeated, older than his years.

"I never wanted any of this," he said quietly. "I want you to know that. I got in too deep, and I couldn't find a way out, and I made terrible choices. But I never wanted to hurt anyone."

Faye met his eyes. "Neither did Margaret. But she's still dead."

Peter had no answer. The officers led him out into the December cold, and the door closed behind him.

The next hour passed in a blur of statements and photographs and officers carefully bagging the documents from Arthur's desk. Faye answered questions until her voice grew hoarse, describing everything—Peter's arrival, his desperation, the struggle, the accidental fire, Tiny's intervention.

Through it all, Tiny stayed pressed against her side, a warm and steady presence. Arthur sat in his chair by the fire, looking exhausted but somehow lighter, as if a weight he'd carried for months had finally lifted.

When the last officer had gone, Luke returned to the study. "I can drive you home," he said. "Officer Davis can drive your Jeep home for you. You've had quite a day."

Faye nodded, suddenly aware of how tired she was. The adrenaline had faded, leaving her hollow and wrung out. "That would be good. Thank you."

She said goodbye to Arthur, who clasped her hands in both of his. "Thank you, Faye. For being brave when I couldn't be."

"You threw that pitcher pretty fast for someone who couldn't be brave."

Arthur's laugh was rusty but real. "Reflex. Forty years of protecting irreplaceable documents." His eyes grew serious. "Margaret would be proud of you. She chose well, trusting you with her research."

"Yes," she said quietly. "She did."

THE DRIVE HOME WAS QUIET. Snow fell in fat, lazy flakes, blanketing Butternut Cove in another layer of white. Christmas lights twinkled from every storefront, and somewhere in the distance, church bells were ringing.

Tiny sprawled across the back seat, taking up every inch of available space, his head resting on his paws. Occasionally his tail thumped against the upholstery—contentment, or maybe just acknowledgment that they were heading home.

Faye watched the familiar streets slide past and felt something loosen in her chest. Not quite peace—not yet—but the possibility of it.

Luke pulled the car to the curb outside her house on Ocean Street. The porch light glowed warm and welcoming, and through the window, Faye could see Dixie moving around in the kitchen.

"I'll come in with you and retrieve the notebook. "Where is it now?" Luke asked.

"Kitchen drawer. Under the dish towels."

"Faye." He turned to face her, his expression serious but not unkind. "You should have told me. But I understand why you didn't. Margaret asked you to protect it, and you did. That complicated your decision making."

"Not having it could have compromised your investigation." Faye admitted.

"It could have." A small smile tugged at the corner of his mouth. "But it didn't. We got him anyway. And now we'll have even more evidence to work with." He paused. "The notebook—it might help us trace the Rosewell connection. Peter's confession gave us a name, but we'll need documentation to build a case. Your grandmother's records might be exactly what we need."

Faye felt something ease in her chest—not absolution, exactly, but something close. "So I didn't completely mess this up?"

"You caught a killer and you and Tiny saved Arthur Whitford's life. I'd say you did okay." Luke's smile widened slightly. "Just maybe next time, instead of the heroics turn the work over to the professionals?"

Faye nodded, "Yes, noted."

They went inside together, Tiny walking between them. Dixie looked up from the stove, her face flooding with relief when she saw Faye.

"Aunt Faye! Mom called—she said there was trouble but didn't know more—are you okay? Is everyone okay?"

"Everyone's fine, sweetheart." Faye pulled her niece into a hug. "It's over. I was with Arthur at his home. Peter Grayson has been arrested. The police have everything they need."

Over Dixie's shoulder, Faye watched Luke retrieve the notebook from the kitchen drawer. He held it carefully, respectfully, as if he understood what it had cost her to give it up.

"I'll be in touch," he said. "Get some rest. Both of you."

He let himself out, and Faye stood in her kitchen, with Dixie in her arms and Tiny leaning on them both. She let herself feel something she hadn't felt in a very long time.

Safe.

Not *fine*—that word had lost its meaning. But safe. Whole. Present.

It was enough. For now, it was enough.

15

Christmas Eve Morning
WEDNESDAY, DECEMBER 24TH.

Faye woke to sunlight streaming through her curtains and the smell of bacon drifting up from the kitchen. For a moment, she lay still, letting the warmth of the blankets and the weight of Tiny's head on her feet anchor her to the present.

It was over. It was really, truly over.

She stretched, and Tiny lifted his head, his tail thumping gently against the mattress in a sleepy greeting.

They'd both earned their rest after yesterday's ordeal—but there was a calm in his dark eyes that hadn't been there before.

We did it. We're safe now.

"Yes, we are," Faye murmured, scratching behind Tiny's ears. "Merry Christmas Eve, my brave boy."

She found Dixie in the kitchen, presiding over a skillet of bacon and a pan of scrambled eggs with the confidence of someone who had been cooking for years rather than weeks. Ebenezer honked a greeting from the back porch, and through the window, Faye could see fresh snow blanketing the yard—a pristine white canvas that sparkled in the morning sun.

"I made breakfast," Dixie announced unnecessarily. "Figured you'd be hungry after, you know. Almost murdered and everything."

Faye laughed—a real laugh, surprising herself with its lightness. "That's one way to put it."

"Evan's coming over later. And Tessa called—she says the café is already packed. People have been lining up since before dawn." Dixie slid a plate across the counter, piled high with eggs and bacon and buttered toast. "Apparently everyone wants to congratulate the woman who caught a murderer."

"Tiny caught the murderer. I just threw some papers at him."

"Same difference." Dixie grinned. "Eat up. You've got a big day ahead."

<hr />

THE HEIRLOOM TABLE *Café* had never looked more festive.

Tessa had outdone herself. Garlands of fresh pine draped the windows, intertwined with cranberry strings and tiny gold bells that chimed whenever the door opened. The Christmas tree in the corner—hastily decorated two days ago—now sparkled with new ornaments, many of them clearly homemade. A hand-painted wooden star crowned the top, and beneath its branches sat a pile of wrapped packages that hadn't been there yesterday.

"What's all this?" Faye asked, stopping just inside the door.

Tessa beamed. "The town's way of saying sorry. And

thank you. And Merry Christmas." She gestured to the packages. "Gifts from your customers. Some of them are from people who weren't very nice to you last week—I think they're feeling guilty."

"They should," Faye said, but there was no anger in it. The anger she'd carried—at the whispers, the cold shoulders, the assumption of her guilt—had faded sometime in the night, replaced by something softer. Understanding, maybe. Or just exhaustion.

The café was indeed packed. Every table was full, and a line snaked from the counter almost to the door. But the atmosphere was different from the past week—warm instead of suspicious, welcoming instead of wary. People smiled at her as she passed. Several reached out to touch her arm, murmuring congratulations and apologies in equal measure.

"Faye!" Mr. Plum, her gruff regular, stood up from his usual corner table. "I owe you an apology. I believed the gossip, and I shouldn't have. You've been nothing but good to this town."

"Thank you, Mr. Plum." Faye squeezed his weathered hand. "That means a lot."

"And your dog!" He looked down at Tiny, who had settled into his usual spot with the dignity of a king returning to his throne. "I heard he tackled that Grayson fellow right to the ground. Wish I'd been there to see it."

Tiny's tail wagged at the attention, and Faye could have sworn she saw pride in those dark eyes.

———

THEY CAME in waves throughout the morning—the people who had doubted her, avoided her, whispered about her behind her back. Some were awkward, stumbling over their words. Others were tearful, genuinely distressed by their own behavior. A few tried to pretend they'd never believed the rumors at all, which Faye found oddly endearing in its transparency.

Mabel Thornton arrived with a basket of homemade preserves and a speech she'd clearly rehearsed. "I was wrong about you, Faye Harper. I let fear cloud my judgment, and I'm sorry for it. These are my grandmother's recipes—fig preserves and spiced pear butter. I hope you'll accept them as a peace offering."

Ivy Chen brought a beautiful calligraphy scroll with Faye's name in elegant brushstrokes. "For your wall," she said shyly. "It means 'courage' in Chinese. Because you have it. More than anyone I know."

Even Beatrice Larkspur, who had been among the coldest in her suspicion. "It will bloom in a few weeks," she said stiffly. "Red flowers. For the New Year." She paused, then added in a rush: "I'm sorry. I should have known better. You have kind eyes—my mother always said you could tell a person's character by their eyes—and I ignored that because I was judgmental."

"Thank you Beatrice, that means a lot."

Rose Fairweather slipped in near the end of the morning rush, without her usual armor of designer clothes and careful composure. She wore a simple wool coat, her dark hair loose around her shoulders.

"I'm not here to apologize," she said, which made Faye smile. "I mean—I am sorry. For not speaking up sooner. For being afraid." She twisted her hands together. "But mostly I wanted to say thank you. For doing what I couldn't. For making sure Margaret's work meant something."

"Margaret did the hard part," Faye said. "She found the truth. We just made sure it came to light."

Rose nodded, her eyes bright. "I'm staying on at the Historical Society. Arthur asked me to help rebuild—to do things properly this time." A small smile crossed her face. "I think Margaret would have liked that."

"I think she would have," Faye agreed.

Faye accepted each apology with grace, each gift with genuine thanks. She understood fear. She understood how it could twist perception, turn neighbor against neighbor. If the past week had taught her anything, it was that community was fragile—and precious. Worth fighting for. Worth forgiving.

By noon, the pile of gifts under the tree had doubled in size, and Faye's heart felt fuller than it had in years.

THE ONE VISITOR she hadn't expected came at half past twelve.

Kent Blake pushed through the café door. His usually immaculate suit was rumpled, his silver hair uncombed, and there were dark circles under his eyes that spoke of sleepless nights and a troubled conscience.

The café went quiet. Every eye turned to watch as Kent crossed to the counter where Faye stood, her hands wrapped around a cup of chai that had long since gone cold.

"Faye." His voice was rough. "Faye. I..." He stopped, swallowed hard, started again. "I've been a fool. A petty, jealous fool. I sabotaged your pudding because I couldn't stand the thought of losing to someone I considered an outsider. And then when everything happened with Margaret, and the police, and the suspicion..." He shook his head.

"You were dealing with being arrested for tampering with evidence," Faye said mildly. "I imagine that took up most of your attention."

Kent's voice cracked. "I've been baking for thirty years. I've won competitions all over New England. But I've never —" He paused, collecting himself. "I've never met anyone who bakes with as much heart as you do. That pudding of yours deserved to win. I knew it the moment I tasted it at the judging. And instead of accepting that gracefully, I tried to tear you down."

The café was utterly silent. Faye could feel dozens of eyes on them, waiting to see what she would do.

She set down her chai cup and extended her hand.

"Apology accepted, Kent. And for what it's worth—your pudding was excellent. The candied fruits were inspired. Maybe next year we could collaborate instead of compete?"

Kent stared at her for a long moment, then shook her hand. His grip was firm, his eyes bright.

"I'd like that," he said quietly. "I'd like that very much."

Someone in the back of the café started clapping. Others joined in, and soon the whole room was applauding—not just for the reconciliation, but for the spirit of forgiveness that Christmas was supposed to be about.

Kent ducked his head, embarrassed but smiling, and retreated to order a coffee. Faye watched him go with a warmth in her chest.

THE LUNCH RUSH had abated and as Faye put the closed sign on the Heirloom Table Café door, Callie Sweet swept in Jaxson as usual was at her heels and Fig draped imperiously around her shoulders. Behind her came Dixie and Evan, holding hands and trying to pretend they weren't, and Dean and Anne Flute, fresh from their hotel and glowing with that particular contentment of people deeply in love.

"There she is!" Callie swept Faye into a hug that smelled of cinnamon and vanilla and home. "The hero of Butternut Cove! I heard you threw legal documents at a murderer like ninja stars."

"That's not quite—"

"And Tiny!" Callie released Faye and bent over to give the Dane a kiss on the head, who accepted the attention with grace. "My magnificent boy! You saved Arthur's life at the Ball AND caught a killer! You're going to be famous. There'll be newspaper articles. Maybe a book deal."

Jaxson barked jealously, and Fig made a sound of regal disdain from Callie's shoulder, as if to remind everyone that *she* had been the one to first sense the danger at the Ball.

"You're all heroes," Faye assured them. "Each of you."

Dean patted her on the shoulder. "We're so proud of you, Faye. When Anne and I heard what happened—He shook his head. "I knew you had grit, but taking on a murderer? That's something else."

"I had help." Faye looked around at all of them—her people, her community, the pets, and her family by choice if not by blood. "I couldn't have done any of it without all of you."

"Speaking of which," Callie said, her eyes sparkling, "we're having Christmas Eve dinner at my place tonight. Everyone's invited. Dean and Anne are going to play carols, I'm making my grandmother's wassail, and there will be enough food to feed an army." She paused. "Or at least enough to feed Jaxson, which is basically the same thing."

Jaxson's tail wagged at the mention of food, his pink tongue lolling happily.

"I'll bring dessert," Faye said. "I think I still have the ingredients for my grandmother's Gingerbread bundt cake."

"Perfect." Callie beamed. "It's going to be the best Christmas Eve Butternut Cove has ever seen."

———

FAYE STOOD ALONE in the quiet café—Tessa had left to prepare for her own family's celebration. She had mention her new beau, David Soales who was flying in from Florida. This was Tessa's Christmas surprise.

Tiny dozed in his wicker chair by the fireplace, long legs folded beneath him.

He lifted his head and fixed her with a long, assessing look.

Yes, Tiny. It's different, isn't it.

I was grateful for your rescue—but I didn't panic. I didn't freeze. I faced it.

I still need you. Just… not in the same way as before.

And you know it. You've always read me better than anyone.

Tiny's tail thumped once in quiet agreement.

Faye gathered her coat, and called Tiny to her side. He was his patient, longsuffering self as she put his red Christmas coat on him. She checked to be certain his festive Christmas glasses were in his coat pocket.

They stepped out together into the Christmas Eve afternoon. The snow had stopped falling, leaving Butternut Cove draped in white.

Lights twinkled in shop windows but they were closing early.

Somewhere nearby, someone was playing "Silver Bells" on a speaker, the melody drifting through the cold, clear air.

She had a cake to bake. A dinner to attend. A family with which to celebrate.

And for the first time in longer than she could remember, Faye Harper felt like she truly belonged.

16

Christmas Eve Night
WEDNESDAY, DECEMBER 24TH.

Callie Sweet's cottage looked like something from a storybook.

Nestled at the end of a winding lane, it glowed with warmth against the winter darkness. Candles flickered in every window. A wreath of fresh evergreen and dried oranges adorned the bright blue door. Smoke curled from the chimney, carrying the scent of wood fire and something delicious— roasting meat, herbs, the unmistakable richness of Callie's famous gravy.

Faye paused at the garden gate, Gingerbread Bundt cake balanced carefully in her arms, and let the scene wash over her. Tiny stood at her side, tail wagging at the familiar smells and sounds drifting from the cottage.

"Ready, honey?" Faye asked.

Tiny's answer was to push through the gate and trot up the path, clearly ready for whatever festivities awaited.

The door flew open before Faye could knock, and Jaxson bounded out to greet them—a golden blur of wagging tail and lolling tongue. He and Tiny touched noses in their customary greeting, then Jaxson led the way inside as if he were the official welcoming committee.

And Callie held the opened door. "You're here!" Callie stepped aside to let the pass. Flushed and happy, an apron covered with Christmas decorations partially hid her festive red dress. "Come in, come in! Everyone else is already in the sitting room. Anne's warming up at the piano, and Dean's been threatening to debut a new song he wrote on the flight over."

The cottage wrapped around Faye like a hug. Low ceilings crossed with dark beams. Walls covered in a cheerful jumble of art and photographs. A fire crackling in a stone hearth that looked as old as the town itself. And everywhere, the small touches that made a house a home—worn quilts draped over chairs, books stacked on every surface, a collection of mismatched teacups displayed on open shelves.

The sitting room was warm and crowded in the best possible way. Dean Flute stood by the fireplace, a glass of Callie's wassail in hand, telling a story that had Dixie and Evan laughing. Anne sat at the upright piano in the corner, running through scales with the easy confidence of a professional. Tessa had claimed the best armchair, her feet tucked up beneath her, looking more relaxed than Faye had seen her in days.

And the animals—oh, the animals. Jaxson had already settled onto his bed by the fireplace. Next to him, Tiny parked himself in his reserved comfy, oversize chair. He sat, his large rear end anchored in the chair while his front paws were planted on the floor. It was a usual Dane moment of gravity as he took in the room and humor as it seemed odd for him to sit like all the other guests. Then Faye looking at the seated Dane remembered his Christmas glasses in his coat pocket and placed them on his head.

Fig observed the proceedings from her perch on the back of the sofa, blue eyes gleaming with genuine amusement.

And Ebenezer, resplendent in a red bow for the occasion, had claimed a spot near the kitchen door where he could supervise both the gathering and the cooking.

"Faye!" Dixie bounced up to take the cake from her hands. "Is this your famous Gingerbread Bundt cake? Would you save us pieces? I need to get my mother up and moving or we will be late to the airport. Dixie turned to the room and called Tessa.

"Hurry up Mom, we're going to be late! Evan is warming up the car and he has already corralled Ebenezer and put him in the back. "We'll drop him—Ebenezer—off at Faye's on the way to the airport."

———

BEFORE DINNER, Dean raised his glass of wassail and called for everyone's attention.

"I know I'm just a visitor here now," he began, his warm baritone filling the room. "But Anne and I have been coming to Butternut Cove for years, and it's always felt like home. Tonight especially."

He looked around at the gathered faces, his expression softening. "When Faye called me last week, I could hear the worry in her voice. The fear. And I thought—how could anyone suspect her? Faye Harper, who never met a stranger she didn't want to feed?"

Soft laughter rippled through the room.

"She didn't just wait for things to work out," Dean continued. "She fought. She asked questions. She put herself in danger to find the truth and protect this town." He raised his glass higher. "So here's to Faye Harper—baker, sleuth in the making, and friend. And to Tiny, the bravest dog I've ever met. May your Christmas be merry, and may next year bring nothing but peace and good pastry."

"To Faye and Tiny!" the room chorused, and glasses clinked in the firelight.

Faye felt tears prick her eyes—the good kind, the grateful kind. "Thank you," she managed. "All of you. I couldn't have done any of it alone."

"That's what friends are for," Callie said simply, squeezing Faye's arm. "Now let's eat before everything gets cold."

———

CALLIE'S CHRISTMAS Eve dinner was a masterpiece of comfort and abundance.

A roast chicken, golden and crispy-skinned, held pride of place on the table. Around it clustered bowls of roasted root vegetables—parsnips and carrots and potatoes, caramelized and fragrant with rosemary. A creamy gratin of winter greens. Warm rolls still steaming from the oven. Cranberry sauce that Callie had made herself from berries picked in the autumn. And the gravy—rich, savory.

"This is incredible," Dean said, reaching for his third roll. "Our family just does pizza on Christmas Eve."

"Nothing wrong with pizza," Callie said warmly. "But I've always loved cooking for a crowd. It's my way of showing love without getting mushy about it."

"You're plenty mushy," Anne teased. "Remember last Christmas when you cried during the dog food commercial?"

"That dog was reunited with his family after being lost for three years!" Callie protested. "Anyone would cry!"

The table erupted in laughter, and even Fig seemed to smile from her spot on the sideboard, where she had positioned herself to keep a watchful eye on the proceedings.

Beside the table, Jaxson and Tiny stood side by side, occasionally receiving scraps from sympathetic hands.

The conversation flowed easily—stories from Dean and Anne's touring days. Lighter topics too: favorite Christmas memories, the best and worst gifts they'd ever received, debate about whether Die Hard counted as a Christmas movie (Dean insisted yes; Anne was scandalized).

Faye let it wash over her, contributing when called upon but mostly content to listen. To witness. To be present in this moment.

AFTER DINNER–AFTER the dishes were cleared and the Gingerbread bundt cake sliced and praised and sliced again— they gathered in the sitting room for music.

Anne took her place at the piano, and Dean pulled up a chair beside her, his guitar across his lap. The fire had burned down to glowing embers, and someone had dimmed the lamps, leaving the room lit mostly by candlelight.

"Any requests?" Dean asked.

"'Silent Night,'" Faye said immediately. "It's not Christmas without 'Silent Night.'"

Anne played the opening notes, soft and reverent, and Dean began to sing. His voice was different here than it was on stage—gentler, more intimate, because he was singing just for them. Anne joined in on the harmonies, her soprano weaving through his baritone like silver thread through gold.

Silent night, holy night...

One by one, the others joined in. Callie's warm alto.

Faye sang too, her voice rusty with disuse but finding its way to the familiar melody. Beside her, Tiny rested his great head on Faye's lap, eyes half-closed in contentment.

Sleep in heavenly peace...

They moved through the old carols— "O Holy Night"

and "The First Noel" and "What Child Is This"—each song a thread in the tapestry of the evening. Between songs, there was quiet laughter, the clink of wassail cups being refilled, the soft crackle of the fire.

At some point, Fig descended from her perch and settled onto Callie's lap, a rare sign of feline approval. Jaxson stretched out before the hearth, his golden fur glowing in the firelight.

"One more," Dean said, adjusting his guitar. "This one's new. Wrote it on the plane, actually. Haven't even played it for our label yet." He glanced at Anne, who nodded encouragingly. "It's called 'The Light Still Shines.'"

He began to play—a simple melody, plaintive and hopeful. And then he sang:

> *When the darkness feels like it might win,*
> *And the cold creeps under your skin,*
> *Look around at the ones who stayed—*
> *The light still shines, don't be afraid...*

Faye's vision blurred with tears. The song was simple, almost childlike in its earnestness, but it spoke to something deep in her—the fear she'd carried all week, the loneliness she'd fought, the relief of finally, finally being seen and believed and loved.

When the last notes faded, the room was silent. Then Callie sniffled loudly and said, "You're going to make me cry again, and I'm still not over that dog food commercial."

Everyone laughed, and the spell broke gently, dissolving into warmth and chatter and the comfortable bustle of friends settling in for the last hours of Christmas Eve.

━━

NEAR MIDNIGHT, the party began to wind down.

Dean and Anne excused themselves. Citing an early flight the next afternoon.

Callie appearing at Faye's elbow with two mugs of hot chocolate.

Faye accepted the mug gratefully. "Thank you for tonight, Callie. For everything."

"Oh, stop." Callie waved a hand. "You're my favorite person to feed. Besides Jaxson, obviously."

They stood in comfortable silence, watching the snow fall beyond the window. Somewhere in the distance, church bells began to ring—midnight, Christmas Day.

"Merry Christmas, Callie," Faye said.

"Merry Christmas, Faye."

Faye gathered her coat, her scarf, her very large dog and his jacket.

"Ready to go home?" she asked Tiny.

Tiny's tail wagged. Always ready.

THE WALK home was quiet and magical.

Snow covered Butternut Cove in a luminous blanket of white under the white crescent moon. Christmas lights glowed in windows. The harbor was still, the boats gently rocking at their moorings. The only sounds were Faye's footsteps.

Faye breathed in the cold, clean air and felt something settle inside her. Peace. Real peace. The kind she hadn't felt in five years.

When she turned onto her street, she was surprised to see lights blazing in her homes windows. She hadn't left them on.

Tiny's tail picked up its steady rhythm, and Faye understood. They had company.

She opened the front door to find Tessa in the kitchen, uncorking a bottle of champagne, with a tall, dark-haired man standing beside her. He had kind blue eyes, a weathered tan, and the easy posture of someone comfortable in his own skin.

"Faye!" Tessa's face lit up. "You're home! I want you to meet someone." She reached for the man's hand. "This is David Soales. We met in Florida last spring. He's... well, he's important in the space program."

David extended his hand with a warm smile. "I've heard so much about you, Faye. Tessa talks about Butternut Cove constantly. I'm starting to understand why."

Faye shook his hand, studying her friend's face. Tessa was practically glowing—not just happy, but settled. Content in a way Faye had not seen in a long time.

"Florida, huh?" Faye raised an eyebrow. "And you kept this a secret?"

"I wanted to be sure," Tessa said softly. "After everything... I needed to know it was real before I brought him home."

Home. The word hung in the air, full of meaning.

"Well," Faye said, taking the champagne flute Tessa offered, "welcome to Butternut Cove, David. And Merry Christmas."

They clinked glasses, the three of them standing in Faye's warm kitchen. Tiny stretched out on his usual spot with a contented sigh. Dixie lifted her glass of Coke in a toast.

"We won't keep you," Tessa said, setting down her glass. "I know you're exhausted. But I wanted you to meet David tonight. It felt right."

"It does," Faye agreed. "It really does."

She hugged Tessa tight—the kind of hug that said everything words couldn't. Then Tessa and David were gone, leaving Faye and Dixie alone in the quiet house.

"I like him," Dixie said from the doorway, where she'd been watching. "He looks at her like she's the best thing he's ever seen."

"He does, doesn't he?" Faye smiled. "Now get some sleep. Christmas morning comes early."

Dixie gave her a quick hug and disappeared upstairs. Faye stood in the kitchen for a moment longer, looking around at the home she'd made. The copper pots hanging above the stove. The herbs drying in the window. The photographs on the refrigerator. The massive dog snoring softly on his sofa by the radiator and there was Ebenezer quietly asleep on the porch who had become a fixture, no longer a guest.

For five years, the answer had been automatic. *I'm fine.* A shield. A performance.

But tonight, Faye Harper knew what it felt like to actually mean it.

She wasn't just fine.

She was home.

17

Christmas Day
THURSDAY, DECEMBER 25TH.

Faye woke to the smell of coffee and the weight of a very large dog on her feet.

Christmas morning. The world made new.

Tiny lifted his head, tail beginning its morning rhythm against the mattress. *Good morning. Are there treats?*

"Merry Christmas to you too," Faye laughed, scratching behind Tiny's ears. "Let's go find out."

She found Dixie already in the kitchen, standing at the stove in candy-cane pajamas, attempting to flip pancakes with varying degrees of success.

"I wanted to surprise you," Dixie said, gesturing at the counter covered in flour, batter drips, and one slightly lopsided stack of pancakes. "Surprise?"

"Best surprise ever." Faye kissed Dixie on the cheek and reached for the coffee pot. "They look perfect."

"They look like pancakes that got into a fight with a spatula," Dixie corrected. "But they taste okay. I tested."

They ate at the kitchen table, Tiny stationed hopefully nearby. The pancakes were indeed a little lumpy, but slathered in butter and maple syrup, they tasted like Christmas morning should taste—warm, sweet, and made with love.

A knock at the door interrupted their second cups of coffee. Faye opened it to find Tessa and David on the doorstep, arms laden with wrapped packages and a basket of pastries.

"Merry Christmas!" Tessa swept in like a festive hurricane. "David and I stopped by *How Sweet It Is*. Callie was doing some Christmas morning baking just us. David already learned that showing up empty-handed is a cardinal sin in Butternut Cove."

"I'm a fast learner," he said with a grin, setting the basket on the counter. "And I've never met a cinnamon roll I didn't like."

They gathered in the living room around the small tree Faye and Dixie had decorated together. The gift exchange was simple but heartfelt—a hand-knitted scarf from Tessa, a book of Florida wildlife photography from David, vintage earrings Dixie had found at a thrift shop. And for Tiny, a new collar tag engraved with his name and Faye's address, because after everything that had happened, everyone agreed he deserved to be properly identified as the hero he was.

⊏⊐

THE KNOCK CAME MID-MORNING, just as Tessa and David were preparing to leave for a walk along the harbor.

Faye answered the door to ten years older than he had a

week ago but dressed carefully in a suit and overcoat, a wrapped package under his arm.

"I hope I'm not intruding," he said, his voice uncertain. "I wanted to thank you properly. And to give you this."

"Not at all. Please, come in." Faye stepped aside to let him enter. "Can I get you anything? Coffee? Tea? What about a cinnamon role?"

"Tea would be lovely but I'll pass on the role. Thank you." Arthur lowered himself into a chair with a grateful sigh. "I won't stay long."

He held out the package, and Faye took it, curious. It was heavier than she expected, wrapped in elegant paper with a silver bow.

"Open it," Arthur urged. "Please."

Inside was a book—old, leather-bound, with gilt lettering on the spine that read *A History of Butternut Cove, 1742-1892.* Faye opened it carefully, and a small card fell out.

For Faye Harper, who understood that the truth matters—even when it's difficult. May you always find the light. —Arthur Whitford

"It was Margaret's," Arthur said quietly. "She loved this book. Read it cover to cover a dozen times. I thought—I thought she would want you to have it."

Faye ran her fingers over the worn leather, feeling the weight of history—both the book's and Margaret's. "Thank you, Arthur. I'll treasure it."

"There's something else." Arthur accepted the tea Dixie brought him, wrapping his hands around the cup as if seeking warmth. "The Historical Society board met this morning—emergency session. We've voted unanimously to approve your application. Welcome to the Butternut Cove Historical Preservation Society, Faye."

Faye stared at him. After everything that had happened—the suspicion, the investigation, the revelation of the board's connection to the conspiracy—she had assumed her application was dead in the water.

"We need people like you," Arthur continued. "People who care about the truth. People who won't look the other way when something's wrong." He managed a tired smile. "Besides, your research on The Heirloom Table Café's original fixtures was genuinely excellent. It would have been approved even without... all the rest."

"I don't know what to say." Faye smiled.

"Say you'll help us do better." Arthur set down his tea. "The society has strayed from its purpose. Charlotte and Oliver—" He shook his head. "They're facing their own consequences now. But the institution can be saved. Should be saved. With the right people leading it."

"I'd be honored to try," Faye said.

Arthur nodded, satisfied. He rose to leave, then paused and sat back down.

"And Sylvie?" Faye asked quietly. "Charlotte's daughter?"

Arthur's expression softened with something like relief—as if he'd been hoping she would ask.

"I reached out to her yesterday. Christmas Eve."

He paused.

"She lives in Jackson Wyoming now—has a family of her own, a career. She's a wildlife photographer. It's a good life, by all accounts."

"How did she take it? The news about Charlotte, about everything?"

"Relieved, I think. Though perhaps not for the reasons you'd expect." Arthur's a sip of tea. "She never wanted the money, Faye. She told Charlotte that from the very beginning —two years ago when she first made contact. She just wanted to know where she came from. Wanted to understand her own history."

"And Charlotte couldn't see past her own fear."

"Couldn't—or wouldn't." Arthur sighed. "My niece has spent her entire life building walls. Protecting the family name, the family fortune, the family reputation. She couldn't understand that Sylvie wasn't a threat to any of those things. She was just a woman looking for answers."

Faye thought of her own walls—the ones she'd built after Derek and Jenny died. The automatic "I'm fine" that had become her armor. She understood, perhaps better than Arthur knew, how fear could make you push away the very things you needed most.

"Will Sylvie come to Butternut Cove?" Faye asked.

"Perhaps someday. We spoke for nearly an hour—she has questions, and I have answers she deserves to hear. But for now, she has her own life to tend to." Arthur smiled, a genuine warmth. "She asked me to send her Margaret's report when it becomes public record. She wants to understand the full truth —not just about the fraud, but about her family. About the choices Charlotte made and why."

"Margaret would have liked that," Faye said softly. "Knowing her work helped someone find the truth they were looking for."

"She would have." Arthur rose again, steadier this time.

"There's something else we should discuss—in the New Year, when things have settled. Your family's connection to the Whitford's. Lot 47." His eyes met hers, and she saw something there—not secrets exactly, but history. Layers of it. "Margaret found more than fraud in those records, Faye. She found a story that's been waiting a long time to be told. Your story, as much as mine."

"I'd like that," Faye said quietly.

"January, then. When Beatrice has gone back to San Francisco, and my old house is quiet again." He smiled—tired but warm. "Some conversations deserve proper time."

18

Chosen Family

THURSDAY, DECEMBER 25TH.

Christmas dinner was a celebration.

They gathered at *The Heirloom Table Café*—closed for business but transformed into a private dining room for Faye's chosen family. Tessa and David had brought champagne. Dixie and Evan had strung fairy lights around the windows. Callie had insisted on contributing three different pies, because choosing just one was apparently impossible.

The table was crowded in the best possible way. Faye at the head, with Tessa and David on one side, Dixie and Evan on the other. Callie had claimed the seat nearest the kitchen, ready to jump up and help at a moment's notice. And at the far end, looking slightly uncomfortable but determined to be present, sat Luke Grayson.

Faye had been surprised when he'd accepted the invitation. Even more surprised by the bottle of wine he'd brought —expensive, carefully chosen, with a card that simply read: *Thank you for not giving up.*

He caught her looking and raised his glass slightly. A small gesture, but it said more than words could.

Luke had brought news beyond Peter's arrest.

"Peter's cooperating," Luke said, accepting a second helping of potatoes. "Naming names. Providing documentation. His lawyer's pushing for a deal—reduced charges in exchange for testimony against the people above him."

"The Rosewell's," Faye said.

"Victor Rosewell and his son Marcus. They run an investment firm out of Boston—Rosewell Capital Partners." Luke's expression was grim. "Turns out Butternut Cove wasn't their first project. The FBI's been building a case against them for years—wire fraud, money laundering, conspiracy. They've done this in at least six other coastal communities. Buy up property through shell companies, manipulate local officials, flip everything to developers."

"Will they be arrested?" Tessa asked.

"It's complicated. Different jurisdictions. Victor's got an army of lawyers." Luke shrugged. "But Margaret's research gave the FBI exactly what they needed to tie the pieces together. She didn't just uncover a local conspiracy—she mapped out an entire criminal enterprise." He raised his glass slightly. "Her work will put Victor Rosewell away. It might take a year, maybe two, but it'll happen."

"She would have liked knowing that," Faye said softly.

"She would have." Luke nodded. "The Bureau's calling it the Margaret Ellis investigation now. Unofficially, of course. But her name's on the file. That matters."

It wasn't perfect justice. Victor Rosewell was still free, still protected by his lawyers and his money. But the wheels were turning. Margaret's work would outlast her—would bring down the people who had ordered her death.

Faye raised her glass. "To Margaret. May the truth she found bring down everyone who tried to bury it."

"To Margaret," they echoed, glasses chiming in the candlelight.

"And Charlotte and her brother Chance," Faye asked quietly.

"Cooperating with investigators," Luke replied. "Arthur convinced them it was the only path forward." Luke shrugged, "they may face charges for the financial crimes—fraud, money laundering.

But they weren't involved in the murders that was all Peter."

It wasn't perfect justice. But it was a movement. And sometimes, that had to be enough.

Faye knew that.

Luke continued, "Charlotte and Chance had been complicit in the scheme that had led to Margaret's death, even if they hadn't wielded the poison themselves. Interestingly, Oliver was not involved. But the wheels of justice turned slowly, and sometimes you had to accept partial victories."

"To Margaret," Callie said, raising her glass. "May she rest in peace, knowing the truth came out."

"To Margaret," they echoed, glasses chiming in the candlelight.

There was also a new face at the table—Kit West, a tech-savvy friend of Tessa's from London who was visiting Butternut Cove after hearing all of Faye's stories. Petite and sharp-eyed, with purple streaks in her dark hair, she had a laugh that filled the room.

"Kit's thinking of relocating," Tessa announced over the appetizers. "Tell them what you do."

"Security consulting," Kit said, reaching for a roll. "Mostly digital—cybersecurity, system audits, that kind of thing. But I've been doing some work with smart home tech and physical security integration too." She grinned. "Basically, I help people figure out who's been snooping where they shouldn't be."

"That would have been useful last week," Callie said dryly.

"Next time you have a murderer to catch, call me first." Kit's eyes sparkled with humor. "I'm very good at finding things people want to stay hidden."

Dixie leaned toward Faye and whispered, "Do you think she's joking?"

Faye wasn't sure.

⸺

AFTER DINNER, the group migrated to the sitting area near the café's fireplace. Someone put on soft music. Dixie and Evan had claimed the loveseat, talking quietly. David and Tessa were examining the vintage photographs on the walls, David asking questions about the town's history while Tessa pointed out landmarks and families.

Faye found herself standing by the window, looking out at the snow-covered square, when Luke appeared beside her with two cups of coffee.

"Thought you might need this," he said, offering one.

"You thought right." She wrapped her hands around the warm cup. "Thank you. For coming tonight. I know it's not exactly... standard procedure."

"No," Luke agreed. "It's not." He was quiet for a moment, watching the snow fall. "But I wanted to be here. You did something remarkable this week, Faye. Most people would have crumbled under that kind of pressure. You didn't."

"I had help."

"You had friends," he corrected. "That's different. Friends support you. But you're the one who had to be brave." He turned to look at her, and something in his expression made her breath catch. "I admire that."

Faye didn't know what to say. The moment stretched between them, full of possibility.

"Well," Luke said finally, clearing his throat. "I should probably head out. Early shift tomorrow. But——" He hesitated. "Maybe we could have dinner sometime. When I'm not investigating you for murder."

Faye laughed, and the tension broke. "I'd like that."

"Good." He smiled——a real smile, warm and slightly uncertain. "Merry Christmas, Faye."

"Merry Christmas, Luke."

She watched him go, feeling something flutter in her chest. Not quite hope. Not quite certainty. But something worth paying attention to.

———

THE PARTY HAD WOUND down to just Faye, Callie, and Kit, lingering over the last of the coffee, when Kit noticed something on the floor near the door.

"Someone dropped this," she said, bending to pick up a small envelope. "Oh——wait. It's addressed to you, Callie."

Callie frowned, taking the envelope. It was yellowed with age, unsealed, with no stamp or return address. Just her name written in elegant, old-fashioned script.

"That's strange," she murmured. "I didn't see anyone leave this."

She turned it over, and Faye saw her freeze.

On the back was a small embossed crest——a circle surrounded by six tiny stars. One of the founding family symbols.

"That's the Sweet family crest," Callie whispered. "My grandmother's family."

Kit leaned in, curious. "What's inside?"

Callie opened the flap with trembling fingers. Inside lay a delicate brass key—old but recently polished—and a slip of paper, brittle with age. Seven handwritten words:

One truth remains. Find what was lost.

Faye studied Callie's face. It wasn't fear there—not even surprise. It was recognition.

"Do you know what this means?" Faye asked.

Callie swallowed. "I think... it means someone believes I'm ready."

"Ready for what?" Kit asked, her security-consultant instincts clearly piqued.

My parents were found dead floating in the water off the cliffs when I was ten. It remains an unsolved mystery." Callie said slowly, still staring at the key.

"Gert, my grandmother, brought me up and left town six months ago." Left me the bakery in her will with no explanation. No forwarding address. She is sailing, and calls now and then."

"She looked up at Faye. "She had secrets. I always knew that. But I was never sure I wanted to know what they were."

"And now?" Faye asked.

Callie slipped the key into her pocket. "Now I think I need to find out."

Kit grinned. "Well. This is much more interesting than the cybersecurity audit I was supposed to be doing next week."

"You might be doing a different kind of research," Faye said, looking at Callie. "If you want help."

"I want help," Callie said immediately. "I definitely want help."

They looked at each other—three women, three very different skill sets, one mystery waiting to be solved.

"Christmas mysteries," Callie murmured, echoing something in Faye's memory.

"The best kind," Faye agreed.

———

LATER–MUCH later—after the café was cleaned and locked and everyone had finally gone home, Faye walked through the snow-covered streets of Butternut Cove with Tiny walking beside her.

The Christmas lights still glowed in windows. The harbor was peaceful, boats gently rocking at their moorings. The world felt hushed and holy in that way that only Christmas night could feel.

She thought about Margaret Ellis, who had died seeking the truth. About Arthur Whitford, who had found the courage to do the right thing even when it cost him his family. About Peter Grayson, who had let fear and desperation drive him to murder. About the Rosewell, still lurking in the shadows, their reckoning yet to come.

And she thought about Callie, standing in the café with that mysterious key in her hand, ready to open a door to her own past.

There would be more mysteries to solve. More challenges to face. The world was full of secrets, and Butternut Cove had more than its share.

But tonight was Christmas. Tonight was for peace, for gratitude, for the simple joy of being alive and surrounded by love.

Faye unlocked her front door and stepped inside, Tiny at her heels. The house was warm. Dixie had left a light on and a note on the kitchen table: *Best Christmas ever. Love you!*

She smiled, hung up her coat, and settled into her favorite chair by the window. Tiny curled up at his sofa by the radiator, already half-asleep. Through the frost-edged glass, Faye could see the harbor lights twinkling in the distance, the dark expanse of the ocean beyond, the endless sky full of stars.

Somewhere out there, a New Year was waiting. New adventures. New beginnings.

But for now—for this perfect, quiet moment—Faye Harper closed her eyes and let herself simply be.

Home. Safe. Loved.

Epilogue: New Year's Day
THURSDAY, JANUARY 1.

The first day of the New Year dawned bright and cold and still over Butternut Cove.

Faye stood on her front porch, parka pulled up around her ears, coffee cup warming her hands, watching the sun rise over the harbor. The water sparkled like scattered diamonds, and the boats bobbed gently at their moorings, their hulls frosted with a light dusting of overnight snow.

A New Year. A fresh start. A blank page waiting to be written.

Tiny nudged her leg with his nose, and Faye reached down to scratch behind his ears. "What do you think, honey? Ready for whatever comes next?"

Tiny's tail wagged. *Always.*

It had been a week since Christmas. A week since Arthur's visit and the mysterious envelope that had appeared for Callie. A week of quiet recovery, of slowly returning to normal—or at least, to whatever passed for normal in Butternut Cove.

The café had reopened on December 22nd to a steady stream of customers. The figgy pudding had become a minor legend—"The pudding that solved a murder," Mabel had called it, which wasn't technically accurate but made for a good story.

Faye sipped her coffee and smiled at the memory. A week ago, she'd been a suspect. Now she was something closer to a local hero. Life had a funny way of turning things around.

———

The New Year's brunch was Callie's idea.

"We need to plan," she'd said on the phone that morning, sounding equal parts excited and nervous. "I've been staring at this key for a week. I can't do it alone."

So now they gathered in Callie's cottage—Faye, Callie, Kit, and Tessa—while Jaxson and Tiny supervised from their spot by the fire and Fig watched judgmentally from her perch on the bookshelf.

Kit had been there a week, having apparently decided that Butternut Cove was more interesting than whatever she'd been doing in Boston. She'd set up what she called a "command center" on Callie's dining table: laptop open, phone charging, a notebook covered in neat handwriting.

"Okay," Kit said, all business. "Let's review what we know."

Callie held up the brass key. It caught the light, gleaming softly. "This was left for me on Christmas Day. No one saw who delivered it. The envelope has my family crest—the Sweet crest, one of the six Butternut Cove founding families."

"And the note," Faye added. "*One truth remains. Find what was lost.*"

My parents' deaths is still an unsolved mystery.

My grandmother, Gert, brought me up.

Six months ago. Left the bakery in my hands left everything to me in a will but no explanation. No forwarding address. Just... gone."

Callie's voice was quiet.

"Well, sort of. She calls now and then. She is sailing around the world. She sounds fine."

"And now someone wants you to find out," Tessa said thoughtfully. "Someone who knew Gert. Someone who's been watching. Waiting until you were ready."

"That's what worries me." Callie turned the key over in her fingers. "What if I'm not ready? What if whatever she was hiding... what if it changes everything?"

Faye reached over and squeezed her friend's hand. "Then we'll figure it out together. That's what we do."

▭

After brunch, Faye and Tessa took a walk along the harbor while Callie and Kit continued their research.

The day was crisp and clear, the kind of winter day that made you grateful for warm coats and good company. Tiny trotted beside them on an easy lead, investigating interesting smells with the dedication of a professional.

"So," Tessa said, linking her arm through Faye's. "How are you really doing?"

Faye considered the question. A month ago, she would have said *"I'm fine"* automatically, without thinking. Now...

"I'm good," she said. "Better than I've been in a long time, actually. Everything that happened—it was terrible, but it also... woke something up in me. I'd been sleepwalking through my life, Tessa. Going through the motions. And now I feel like I'm actually living again."

Tessa nodded. "I noticed. There's a light in your eyes that wasn't there before." She paused. "It suits you."

They walked in comfortable silence for a moment, watching the boats sway gently in the harbor.

"David is going back to Florida next week," Tessa said finally. "But he's coming back. We're going to try... something. I don't know what to call it yet. But it feels right."

"I'm glad." Faye smiled at her friend. "You deserve something that feels right."

"So do you." Tessa's eyes sparkled with mischief. "Speaking of which—how was dinner with Detective Grayson yesterday?"

Faye felt her cheeks warm. "It was just dinner."

"Uh-huh. And the fact that he asked you to dinner again next week?"

"How did you—" Faye stopped. "Dixie told you."

"Dixie tells me everything." Tessa grinned. "So?"

"So... I said yes." Faye couldn't help the smile. "But it's early. Very early. And after everything with the investigation, it's complicated. He's being careful. I'm being careful. We're both being careful."

"Sometimes careful is good," Tessa said. "Sometimes careful means you're building something that lasts."

Faye thought about that. Building something. She liked the sound of it.

━━

That evening, as the sun set over Butternut Cove in streaks of orange and pink, the four women gathered one last time in Callie's sitting room.

Kit had made progress. The key, she'd determined, was old—probably turn of the century—and appeared to fit a specific type of lock commonly used on safety deposit boxes and private vaults.

"The question is," Kit said, closing her laptop, "what was Gert Sweet protecting? And where did she hide it?"

"The bakery," Callie said slowly. "It has to be the bakery. She left it in my care me for a reason."

"Then that's where we start." Faye leaned forward. "Tomorrow. First thing."

"I'm in," Tessa said.

"Obviously I'm in," Kit added. "This is way better than debugging corporate firewalls."

Callie looked around at her friends—these women who were dropping everything to help her chase a mystery she didn't fully understand. Her smiled at them with gratitude.

"Thank you," she said. "All of you. I don't know what I'd do without you."

"You'd figure it out," Faye said. "But you don't have to. That's the point."

They raised their glasses—hot cider this time with cinnamon—and clinked them together.

"To the New Year," Callie said.

"To new mysteries," Kit added.

"To new beginnings," Tessa offered.

"To friends," Faye finished. "Old and new."

Outside, the first stars of the New Year began to appear, scattered across the darkening sky like promises waiting to be kept.

Later, walking home with Tiny through the quiet streets, Faye thought about the year ahead.

There would be Arthur's revelations about her family's connection to the Whitford's—that mysterious mention of Lot 47 and a story waiting to be told. There would be Luke, and whatever was growing slowly between them. There would be Callie's connecting dots, Kit's sharp mind, and Tessa's steady presence.

There would be the café, and the Historical Society, and the simple daily rhythms of life in a small town. There would be figgy pudding and cinnamon rolls and coffee brewing at dawn and steaming cups of chai. There would be Tiny, loyal and brave, by her side through whatever came next.

And there would be mysteries. Butternut Cove had shown

her that much. Beneath its picturesque surface, the town held secrets—generations of them, waiting to be uncovered.

She thought about the six founding families: the Whitfords, the Ellises, the Sweets, the Martins, the Doyles, and the Harpers. So much history. So much still hidden.

The year was new. The page was blank. And whatever came next, Faye Harper was ready.

THE END

Faye, Callie, Kit, and Tessa will return

The next chapter of Butternut Cove's story is already taking shape…

What is Figgy Pudding

Figgy pudding—also called Christmas pudding—is a traditional British holiday dessert, rich with dried fruit, warm spices, and history. Despite the name, it isn't a cake. It's a steamed pudding, served warm and often finished with custard, cream, or a splash of brandy.

In many families, figgy pudding is made well ahead of Christmas—weeks or even months before—with the belief that time deepens its flavor. The pudding waits quietly, maturing as the season approaches, until it's finally brought out to be shared.

In *Butternut Cove*, figgy pudding carries more than holiday comfort. It reflects the way the past lingers beneath the present, how traditions—and secrets—are carried forward, and how truth, like good pudding, often benefits from patience.

A Simple Figgy Pudding (For Curious Bakers)

This is a gentle, home-style version of figgy pudding—less a strict recipe and more a tradition passed along.

You'll need:

- mixed dried fruit (raisins, currants, chopped dates or figs)
- brown sugar
- breadcrumbs or flour
- butter
- warm spices (cinnamon, nutmeg, cloves)
- a splash of brandy or rum (optional)
- eggs
- milk

The dried fruit is soaked ahead of time—sometimes for hours, sometimes for weeks—then mixed with the remaining ingredients to form a thick, rich batter. The pudding is steamed until dark and fragrant, then set aside until Christmas, when it's reheated and served warm.

No two families make figgy pudding the same way. That's part of the tradition.

Stay a Little Longer
in Butternut Cove

Thank you for visiting Butternut Cove.

If you loved the town, the people, and the secrets weaving through its history, you don't have to say goodbye just yet.

I've created a special bonus for readers who want to linger —featuring behind-the-scenes details about Butternut Cove, its founding families, and a few extras I couldn't fit into the story.

Join my reader list here to receive your free bonus and be the first to hear about new mysteries set in Butternut Cove.

Click for your bonus

I'll only write when there's something worth sharing.

About Naomi Greer

Naomi Greer writes cozy mysteries set in small towns where community matters, secrets linger, and even holiday traditions can hide unexpected twists.

When she isn't imagining life in Butternut Cove, Naomi enjoys sea air, strong tea, and stories where kindness and curiosity go hand in hand.

To learn more about Naomi's books or stay connected, visit Butternut Cove

www.ingramcontent.com/pod-product-compliance
Lightning Source LLC
Chambersburg PA
CBHW071331250626
47159CB00004B/1554

* 9 7 8 1 9 4 1 4 8 6 1 4 6 *